In that moment, he knew he had to address the attraction crackling between them. If he didn't speak up, there was no way they'd be able to work together every day. Before he could get his speech off the ground, though, she spoke.

"Mr. Alvarez, I think it's better if we address this now."

His brow hitched. "You mean, the attraction between us?"

She nodded, her gaze drifting up to meet his. "You're a handsome man, and I would be lying if I said I wasn't attracted to you."

He could feel the smile curling his lips. "I won't deny how I feel about you, either."

"And how is that?"

"Like a schoolboy with a crush." It was an honest answer, and the best way he could think of to describe the way he felt whenever she entered his space.

She moved in, closing the space between them. A sly smile graced her full lips. "Oh, really."

"Really." He raised his hand, letting his knuckle graze the soft skin of her jaw. She trembled, but didn't back away or reject his touch.

Dear Reader,

Yay! It's finally time for the "Latin Lover" of the Queen City Gents to meet his match. I'm so happy that you've picked up a copy of *A Sultry Love Song*, and I'm so excited to share this story with you. As much as I love writing stories set in my home state, in this book, I got to stretch a little bit because the hero and heroine are going to the sunny shores of Costa Rica. Talk about an exotic location—and it just happens to be the home of Marco Alvarez, the story's hero. He and Joi Lewis share an undeniable attraction, and I hope you'll enjoy the ride!

Remember, I love hearing from readers, so feel free to contact me via the form on my website, or on social media (I'm KiannaWrites on Facebook, Twitter and Pinterest).

All the best,

Kianna

A Sultry Love Song

Kianna Alexander

HARLEQUIN® KIMANI™ ROMANCE

Recycling programs
for this product may
not exist in your area.

ISBN-13: 978-0-373-86475-1

A Sultry Love Song

For questions and comments about the quality of this book please contact us
at CustomerService@Harlequin.com.

HARLEQUIN®
www.Harlequin.com

Printed in U.S.A.

Kianna Alexander, like any good Southern belle, wears many hats: loving wife, doting mama, advice-dispensing sister and gabbing girlfriend. She's a voracious reader, an amateur seamstress and occasional painter in oils. Chocolate, American history, sweet tea and Idris Elba are a few of her favorite things. A native of the Tar Heel State, Kianna still lives there with her husband, two kids and a collection of well-loved vintage '80s Barbie dolls.

Books by Kianna Alexander

Harlequin Kimani Romance

This Tender Melody
Every Beat of My Heart
A Sultry Love Song

Visit the Author Profile page at Harlequin.com for more titles.

In Loving Memory of My Sweet Grandmother,
Lily Mae Edwards Mckinnon, 1933–2016.

Acknowledgments

A Sultry Love Song presented some very unique research opportunities for me, in that it allowed me to explore some aspects of Costa Rican culture. It also allowed me time to look briefly into the lives of two jazz saxophone pioneers: Charlie Parker and John Coltrane. Hopefully, these details are woven into the story so seamlessly that you won't realize it until you've finished the book :).

I'd like to thank my husband for allowing me the space and time to write. I'd also like to thank the wonderful ladies of the Destin Divas group, whose talent and insight helped get me over the hump when this story was still in its early stages. I won't name all twenty-five women but you know who you are and you ladies ROCK! Also, another shout-out to my Council of Queens, and to Beverly Jenkins, who continues to take my calls and dole out the best advice on writing and life. I have some amazing people in my life, who make me feel truly special.

Chapter 1

Joi Lewis shimmied over to her desk, the sounds of Kool & the Gang pouring from her computer's speakers. The music filled her small office inside Citadel Security, the company she'd founded eight years ago. The late-morning sunshine flooding through her vertical blinds cast a glow on the cluttered surface of her desktop, and she chided herself for neglecting to clear it off—again. Since she needed to do the books for the previous month, there would be no more putting it off. So, with music to motivate her, she began digging through the mountain of papers, magazines and random items piled up on the black lacquer desktop.

Karen, Joi's college classmate and business partner, poked her head into the office. Joi gave her a nod. She could see Karen's lips moving, but she had no idea what she was saying. She continued to go about the task of cleaning the desk.

Karen started flailing her arms, to signal Joi to pay attention.

Joi finally looked up, still dancing. "What?"

Karen rolled her eyes, then cupped her hands around her mouth. "Turn down that music, please!"

Joy twisted the knob on her computer speaker and gave her partner a sheepish grin. "Sorry. Music makes things go by faster."

Karen shook her head, folding her arms across her chest. Tall and curvy, Karen Russell controlled the cybersecurity aspects of Citadel's business. She wore a peach knee-length sheath that hugged her figure and complemented her complexion, accessorized with several pieces of gold jewelry. Despite her ultra-feminine looks, Karen was as big a computer nerd as they came. "You know, you could just tidy it up at the end of each day. That way it wouldn't get so out of hand."

Joi waved her off. "You sound like my mom. Go do something technical while I finish this."

"Aren't you supposed to be working on the October profit and loss statement?" Karen leaned against the door frame, awaiting an answer.

"Yes, and I will as soon as I get my desk clear. So, shoo."

Karen shrugged. "Call me when you're done."

After Karen had left, Joi looked down at the uniform she wore every day: a pair of black slacks and a white button-down blouse embroidered with Citadel's logo. While her position as owner left her free to wear anything she pleased, she chose to wear the same uniform her security guards wore. In her mind, it made sense. Plus, she didn't spend nearly as much time as Karen did fussing over an outfit. That left her more free time to work, and to help raise Citadel's profile in the community.

By the time the playlist finished half an hour later, she'd culled most of the unneeded items from her desktop. Ready to take advantage of the newfound space, she sat down in her black leather executive chair. She opened her accounting software and dove into the reports displayed on-screen.

It took less than twenty minutes for her to discover a serious problem. Her face creased into a frown, and she called out for Karen.

Karen strolled in from her office in the next room. "What's up? Are you done running reports?"

Joi curled her finger in Karen's direction. "Come over here and look at this."

Karen dragged a folding chair next to where Joi sat, and joined her in peering at the figures that were displayed on the screen.

After a few moments of silence, Karen asked, "Are these numbers right?"

With a slow nod, she responded, "Yes. I've checked them three times." While she didn't maintain a pristine office, she did keep meticulous financial records.

In typical fashion, Karen grabbed the blond highlighted ends of her ponytail and began twisting them. "Crap."

"Crap is right." Joi turned away from the screen to look at her friend and business partner. "Losing that contract in September has had a bigger impact on our bottom line than we thought." One of their small business clients, Wilma Clark, had retired and closed up her small boutique, leaving two of the guards without a regular assignment. The boutique sold designer shoes and accessories to Charlotte's wealthier citizens. Mrs. Clark requested the guards after a break-in at the store. "It looks like Mrs. Clark's last check to us bounced."

A frown creased Karen's brow. "That's not like her. She was one of our first clients, and she's never written us a bad check."

"I know." Joi shrugged. She knew Mrs. Clark well enough to know that the bounced check hadn't been some malicious attempt at defrauding Citadel. "To be honest, I don't feel right pursuing her for the money, either. She was such a good client, and now that she's retired, she's much less likely to be able to pay it anyway."

"I agree." Karen sat back in her chair, let out a soft sigh. "Is she even still in the area?"

"I don't really know. She did mention having a son in Florida. But I haven't seen her since she shut the boutique down, and that was three weeks ago." Joi hadn't really thought to question Mrs. Clark about how she'd be spending her retirement.

"So what are we going to do?"

The two of them sat in uncomfortable silence for a few moments.

Finally, Karen gave voice to what they were both thinking. "If we don't get another client quick, we are going to be out of business."

A long sigh escaped Joi's mouth. "We've got enough for payroll, and to keep the lights on for now, but not much more. We've got to drum up some business."

Standing, Karen refolded her chair and tucked it

into the back corner of the room. "I'm on it. I'm going to see what I can do to revamp the website, and to get us some social media attention." She was out the door by the time she finished her sentence.

That was what Joi loved about Karen. They both shared an equal amount of passion for Citadel. Whatever the task, Joi knew Karen would always put in the necessary effort to accomplish their business goals. She couldn't imagine what Citadel would be without her brainy college classmate as her partner.

And while Karen did the technical thing she was so good at, Joi planned to kick it old-school, and solicit some business using the tried-and-true method she preferred. Taking her desk phone out of its cradle, she opened her contact file on the computer and started to dial.

She spent the next hour going through her contacts, making calls and putting people on notice that Citadel now had an open slot for a new client. A few people said they would follow up with her within the week, but some flatly conveyed their disinterest. When she replaced the handset in the cradle, she leaned back in her chair and blew out an exasperated breath. Prospecting was the one aspect of running a business she didn't care for, but she would do whatever it took to keep her company up and running.

Citadel was so much more than just her work. It was the realization of her dreams. She thought back to the fateful day in high school when she'd blacked a boy's eye for calling her older sister a giraffe. Her mother had told her to find a way to turn her so-called aggression into a business, and she'd decided she wanted to own a security firm. She'd worked hard to get here, not just for herself, but for the women she worked with. One of her company's policies was to hire female guards with a background in military or police work. While that policy dissuaded some businesses from contracting with Citadel for their security needs, Joi was proud of her business and everything it stood for. The former police officers and female veterans she employed as guards were just as capable as their male counterparts, and she would vouch for their abilities anytime, without hesitation.

A loud grumbling sound from her stomach reminded her of her need for food and pulled her out of her thoughts. Rising from the desk, she grabbed her red peacoat from the coatrack, and prepared to face the chilly November winds in pursuit of lunch.

With one hand in the pocket of his slacks, Marco Alvarez stood by his office window. His other hand held a mug filled with strong black coffee he sipped from as he viewed the cold gray November day. The frost clouding the glass pane reminded him of just how chilly it was out there, and how much he dreaded going back outside later in the day.

The chiming of an incoming video call split the quiet of the room, drawing his attention to the computer monitor atop his desk. Coffee in hand, he sat down in his desk chair and clicked the mouse to answer the call. "Good morning, Sal. How are you?"

The video window showed an image of Salvatore Perez. As president and chief executive officer of Royal Bank and Trust, Sal was about as serious as a man could be, but he always managed a smile for his childhood buddy. "I'm good, Marco. And how is the weather over there?"

Marco felt the frown crease his brow as he glanced back to the frosty window. "It's deceptively sunny, and a sweltering forty degrees out there." Even though he'd been living in the United States for over a decade, he still hadn't adjusted to the cool weather that gripped the Southeast from November to January. Knowing that the Charlotte area was considerably warmer than points in the northern part of the country provided little comfort on chilly days like this one.

Sal chuckled, straightening his bright red tie. "I'm sure you know it's beautiful here in Limón. Sunny, cloudless blue skies and temps in the seventies." His gray eyes held a twinkle of amusement.

Marco groaned aloud.

In response, Sal chuckled again. "Homesick, my friend?"

"You know I am. I haven't been home in almost three years." Hearing his friend describe the gorgeous weather in his coastal hometown of Limón, Costa Rica, only made him homesick. "Stop torturing me, Sal, and get to the reason why you called."

Sal's smile faded a bit as he returned to his businesslike demeanor. "Right. I wanted to see how much progress you've made in hiring a permanent security firm for the Charlotte branch."

Marco ran a hand through his straight dark locks. "Not as much as I'd hoped. I've had a few proposals, but so far none have moved me."

"You know, the board members and I agree that the bank is well established now, and that it's time to bring on a private, dedicated security staff."

Marco nodded. "I agree. Frankly, I'm tired of dealing with the temp agencies. The branch has more than enough depositors now to justify hiring permanent security." The Charlotte branch, where Marco served as president and executive of operations, had been open for five years. During that time, thousands of accounts of all types had been opened there, for both business and personal use. Other than a branch in New York City, it was the only branch on the East Coast. Royal Bank and Trust was an international company, with five worldwide branches, and Marco was proud that his branch was thriving despite its smaller market.

Sal sat back in his chair. The fabric of his dark suit crinkled as he rested his elbows atop his desk and tented his fingers. "I'll need you to hire someone ASAP, within a week if possible. Can I count on you, Marco?"

He knew it would be a stretch, but he still felt confident he could get it done. "Sure, Sal. I'm on it."

"Oh, and one more thing. Be mindful of the budget. The board has approved a yearly amount for the contract, and you should be careful not to accept a bid that will exceed it."

"Got it. Anything else, Sal?"

"Not at the moment. But I'll check back in with you at the end of next week. Have a good day, Marco."

"You, too."

The video call ended and the screen faded to black. As quiet settled over his office again, Marco wondered how he was going to find a security firm to take on the job of protecting his bank branch. If it were left solely up to him, he would have sought a private security firm much earlier. But the board's primary concern was that the branch met certain profitability goals first. When the Charlotte branch had hit the benchmark for the fiscal year ending this past summer, Marco had been thrilled.

He'd been looking for a firm for almost a month, and now he had only a few days to find someone. It would be a difficult feat to accomplish, but Marco had set his mind to more difficult things and succeeded. He was determined not to disappoint the board, or Sal. He felt extremely fortunate to have such a good working relationship with him. Sal knew him better than most people in his life, and was the closest thing he'd had to a brother while growing up in Costa Rica.

Marco picked up his hands-free headset and put it on. He figured his best bet was to call up his friends and colleagues in the local financial sector and see if anyone could offer a recommendation. The size of his budget for the contract dictated that he'd need a smaller, local firm as opposed to a state- or nation-wide one.

After seventy solid minutes of making calls, Marco removed his headset and looked at the names of the three firms he'd jotted on a notepad atop his desk. He used the intercom system to buzz his branch manager.

A few moments later, Roosevelt Hunter opened the office door and entered. Roosevelt, a tall, fit black man in his fifties, was Marco's next in command. "What do you need, Marco?" Having been employed at the branch since it opened, Roosevelt had finally started calling Marco by his first name, as he'd requested from day one.

Marco tore the top sheet from his notepad, and handed it to the branch manager. "Roosevelt, could you contact these three security firms and solicit proposals from them?"

Taking the offered paper, Roosevelt nodded. "I'm on it. What day do you want them to come in?"

Marco scratched his chin. "If anyone can have their proposal drawn up and ready to present tomorrow after lunch, let them know they'll have a leg up."

One of Roosevelt's brows rose. "You mean you want to sit through security proposals on a Friday afternoon?"

Marco chuckled. "Not really, but I'm on a tight deadline here, so I don't have much of a choice."

Roosevelt gave him a mock salute. "Whatever you say, boss. I'll get right on it." He turned and left the office, closing the door behind him.

Marco glanced at his gold wristwatch. It was a quarter till one, but he'd become accustomed to taking his lunch later than most. He didn't have any desire to go out, so he grabbed his smartphone and placed a call to have his food delivered. After he hung up, he eased his chair closer to the desk, and started on the stack of paperwork on the desk awaiting his signature.

After all, the forms weren't going to sign themselves.

Chapter 2

Friday morning, Joi's efforts in reaching out to her business contacts paid off in the form of a phone call to the office. She smiled through the entire call, and by the time she hung up with the man on the other end, she was pretty sure she'd found the perfect opportunity to get Citadel operating in the black again.

She called out for Karen, who was working in her office next door.

"We only have a few hours to pull together a proposal."

Karen's brow hitched, her face reflecting her confusion. "A proposal for what?"

"I just spoke to a Mr. Roosevelt Hunter, the branch manager at Royal Bank and Trust. They're looking for a new security contractor, and apparently someone recommended us."

Karen's confusion melted into a smile. "Great. But why don't we have more time to get the proposal together?"

Joi shrugged. "Mr. Hunter says they're on a tight deadline to make a choice, and that if we could make our pitch this afternoon, it would give us a major advantage."

"What time is your appointment?"

"Two o'clock." Joi noted her business partner's emphasis of the word *your*. Karen was many things: fashionable, organized and extremely intelligent. She was also pretty shy, which meant she never accompanied Joi to things like this. Karen much preferred to be left alone with her computer.

Leaning against the door frame, Karen spoke again. "Gather your stuff and meet me in the conference room."

Karen disappeared, and Joi got up and began to gather the supplies they would need. When she had everything tucked into the wheeled caddy she kept by her desk, she took it down the short hallway to the small conference room at the end.

The black lacquer table centering the room seated six people. Each of the four corners held a live fern in a wicker planter. Vertical blinds covered the tall windows on one side of the room.

Karen was already seated at one end of the table when Joi walked in. "When are we going to hang some pictures or something in here?"

Joi glanced at the blank, aqua-hued wall opposite the window. Sliding into her seat next to Karen, she shrugged. "I don't know. I thought the bright-colored paint was decoration enough."

A few moments later, they laid their paper and pens out on the table, and began the process of drawing up a proposal. As they conversed about what they would offer Royal, Joi took notes in a small notebook, while Karen typed away at the keys of her laptop.

As morning turned into afternoon, Karen finished the proposal, and hit Send to print the document via the office's wireless printer. After Joi retrieved it, she deposited the papers into a navy-and-yellow folder with the Citadel logo emblazoned on the front of it. "This is it, Karen. This is the winning bid on that bank contract."

Karen stood, stretching her arms over her head. "I hope you're right. Can we break for lunch now?"

Glancing at her phone, Joi nodded. "We need to. It's a quarter after twelve, and I gotta have time to eat, freshen up and drive over to the bank before my appointment."

Karen moved past her. "I'll hang out here and order in. Go on and grab lunch, then go knock 'em dead."

"Thanks, Karen." Joi spent a few minutes making sure she had everything she'd need for the afternoon, then departed.

A little over an hour later, she pulled her black single-cab pickup truck bearing the Citadel logo into a space behind Royal Bank and Trust. She'd stopped in the restroom of the diner she'd had lunch in to change. Forgoing her usual uniform, she'd chosen a pair of gray wool trousers and a matching blazer, paired with a bright red blouse. As she exited her truck and faced the chilly November wind, she was grateful for the warmth of the outfit. Moving across the lot as quickly as she could in her high-heeled red leather booties, she entered the building with the proposal tucked beneath her arm.

She looked around the interior of the bank, familiarizing herself with the layout. Knowing the lay of the land would be the first step in protecting the bank's assets. She took a few moments to walk the perimeter of the space. The bank's lobby was reasonably large, considering the size of the building as it appeared from the outside. It was also pretty typical of a bank. A central desk staffed by three tellers at separate windows, a set of tall tables to the left side of the entrance stocked with forms and pens, and a waiting area to the right. A glass wall separated a corridor from the open lobby, accessed by a set of double doors. In the corridor were two small offices belonging to the bank's branch manager and loan officer, according to the signs on the doors.

Joi wandered over to the narrow hallway beyond the offices, to where she assumed the vault was located. Just as she approached the round metal disk-shaped door, someone tapped her on the shoulder.

Joi whirled around, poised to act.

A chocolate-skinned man of average height stood there. Apparently he sensed her agitation, because he took a large step back as he spoke. "I'm Roosevelt Hunter. Are you Ms. Lewis?"

She relaxed her stance right away. "Yes, I am." She stuck her hand out. "Nice to meet you, Mr. Hunter. Sorry about that."

Roosevelt offered a smile. "It's fine. Impressive reflexes, Ms. Lewis."

Inside she was mortified, but outwardly she smiled. "Thank you."

"Mr. Alvarez is ready to see you."

Joi followed the branch manager as he led her farther down the hallway she'd been exploring. Turning a corner they came to a sizable office. The glass-paned door to the office stood open.

With a nod to Mr. Hunter, Joi stepped inside the office, with her free hand extended. "Good afternoon, Mr. Alvarez. I'm…"

The dark-haired man seated behind the desk looked up. His bronzed face held eyes that were dark, assessing and familiar.

Fixing her with a piercing gaze, he stood to his full height and cut her off midsentence. "I know who you are."

Marco stared at the woman standing in front of his desk, torn between disbelief and irritation. Could the woman who'd abandoned his friend Ernesto at the altar really be there, in his office?

"I, um. I…" she stammered, as if she were still attempting to identify herself.

He folded his arms over his chest, taking in the sight of her shapely, smartly dressed form. "Like I said, I know who you are. Why are you here, Joi?"

She seemed to recover her professional demeanor then. She tucked her shoulders back and stood tall. "It's two o'clock. I am the owner of Citadel Security, and we have an appointment."

"Is that so?" He felt his brow furrow. If someone in full makeup and a clown suit had shown up for the appointment, he would have been less surprised.

"Yes, and if you don't mind, I'd like to make my presentation." She handed him a dark blue folder. When he opened it, he found several pages of neatly typed facts and figures.

His eyes drifted from the carefully prepared report and back to her face. Her earlier discomfort had disappeared, leaving behind nothing but confidence. If she were intimidated by his standoffish manner, she didn't let on.

He returned to his seat, straightened his tie. "Yes, Ms. Lewis. Go ahead." If she could keep things strictly business, then so could he. Based on her demeanor, his expectations for her proposal were very high.

Mindful of the edict he'd received from Sal, Marco paid close attention to Joi's presentation. He took a few moments to leaf through the pages inside the folder she'd given him, which provided a written representation of everything she was saying. He noted how astute she was, and how thorough a vision she had for serving Royal's security needs. He also noticed the way the soft fabric of her suit hugged the lines of her body, which was far curvier than it had been six years prior. Looking at her now made it seem as if that had been a lifetime ago.

Feeling a building warmth in the room, he loosened his tie. He watched her glossy, cherry-red lips move as she spoke.

Her mouth stopped moving, and she watched him, an expectant look spread across her face. Suddenly, he realized she'd asked him a question. "Pardon me?"

"I asked if you had any questions for me, Mr. Alvarez." Annoyance registered in her expression, only for a moment, before she returned to her convivial smile.

Drawing his focus away from her appearance, he sat back in his chair and tented his fingers. "You've given a thorough proposal, and I'm impressed. The only thing I need to know now is your bid."

She quoted him the amount.

His brow hitched in surprise. Her bid was within a few thousand dollars of the budget the board had approved for him. Only one other company had bid today, and their offer had so far exceeded the budget, Marco already knew he wouldn't be calling them back. By his own honest assessment, if Citadel could deliver all the benefits that Joi had promised, Royal would be getting them for a steal.

"How does that sound to you, Mr. Alvarez?"

He was thrilled, but he knew better than to reveal that in a business negotiation. Tempering his reaction, he offered a slow, noncommittal nod. "I think it's a reasonable offer." Since she was still standing, and he planned to draw the encounter out a bit more, he gestured to the guest chair near her. "Please, have a seat."

With a curt shake of her head, she replied, "I prefer to stand."

He had to assume she was making a show of dedication, or of stamina. Something told him that even with the specter of their past history hanging between them, she was too serious about her business to let anything petty interfere with their interactions.

Deciding he'd test that, he asked her, "What have you been up to these past few years, Ms. Lewis?"

Her lovely brown face crinkled a bit. "I'm sorry, but I don't understand what that has to do with my proposal."

He shrugged. "I'm simply curious as to what path you took after we parted, and how it brought you into my presence again."

She blinked a few times, her soft brown eyes darting around the interior of his office. "I took a few continuing education classes and opened an office for my security firm. Basically, I've been working on my dream since the last time I saw you."

He thought back on those days, when he'd known a totally different Joi Lewis than the one standing before him now. But she'd always been tough, and that hadn't changed. "I see."

As if she sensed where the conversation was headed, she squared her shoulders. "Let me level with you, Mr. Alvarez. I know you may have a negative opinion of me, due to what happened in the past. But I stand behind my decision, and I hope you'll respect me enough as a professional that you won't let that incident affect your decision."

He watched her, noting that she'd only referred to her abandonment of Ernesto at the altar as an "incident." It came across a little crass, but she was right. They were both professionals, and it would be unethical and ill-advised for him to flatly deny Citadel's bid because of something that had happened years ago.

A few silent moments passed with each of them assessing the other.

Finally, he spoke. "Ms. Lewis, I'm not going to allow anything to shape the decisions I make for Royal, except for my best judgment of what is most beneficial to the company."

She nodded, keeping her expression flat.

"I noticed in your material that Citadel has an all-female staff. Why is that?"

"My guards are all accomplished women, decorated military veterans or experienced former law enforcement officers. Despite their credentials, it's difficult for them to find work. I aim to remedy that."

"Out of altruism?" He watched her, anticipating her answer.

She held his gaze. "Out of good business sense."

He offered a smile, impressed by her savvy. "That's why I'm going to offer Citadel the contract right now. But be aware, your company will need to complete a thirty-day trial period, and if for any reason I or my branch manager are dissatisfied, we'll have to rescind our offer."

For the first time since she'd stepped into his office, she gave him a full, genuine smile. The wide spread of her ruby lips showed off two rows of pearly-white teeth. "I understand completely. Thank you, Mr. Alvarez. Citadel will go above and beyond your expectations, I promise."

He stood, moved around the side of his desk, with his hand extended toward her.

She approached him, shook his hand.

He knew that this was an everyday gesture in business, merely a sign of good faith to seal their professional agreement. Logic told him their handshake would be just like any other he shared with an associate during the course of his day at work.

But the moment his hand closed around hers, he felt something. It was subtle, but undeniable, like a charge of static electricity running up his arm. He looked down at their joined hands. The softness of her skin, along with her feminine fragrance wafting toward his nostrils, made him feel like an awkward teen who'd just scored a date with the head cheerleader.

The moment lengthened. They'd already shaken

hands, but for some reason, he hesitated to release his grip.

When he let his gaze rise to her face, he could see the flush of heat making its way up from the column of her throat and into her nut-brown cheeks. She was, in one word, stunning.

She cleared her throat, breaking the spell of the moment.

He released her hand, and took a step back to give her some personal space.

"If there's nothing else, I really need to get back to the office and prepare my employees." She'd already moved back to where she'd been standing.

"There's nothing more at the moment." He uttered the words while he watched her stoop to pick up her purse from the floor. The soft fabric of her slacks stretched around her full hips, and his pleasure at the sight caught him so off guard. He turned away.

"I'll return with my guards bright and early Monday morning." She moved toward the door, but stopped there to await his direction.

He shook his head. "Tuesday. Monday is Veterans Day, and the bank will be closed."

"Got it. I'll see you then. And thank you again, Mr. Alvarez." She blessed him with another slight smile before disappearing through the open office door.

Returning to his seat behind the desk, he looked at the open folder she'd left him. He promised himself he would go over the documents again later, when he wasn't so distracted and out of sorts.

After today's interaction with Joi, he wondered if "distracted" was about to become his default state.

Chapter 3

That evening, Joi and Karen took all eight of their employees out to celebrate winning the security contract for Royal Bank and Trust. The women were now seated around a large table in the rear of Mimosa Grill, enjoying their meals and each other's company.

Joi looked around at the faces of the women. Their workplace sisterhood was something she cherished, because it made doing what she loved that much better.

With that in mind, she stood and tapped her water glass with the tines of a fork. "I'd like to make a toast."

The women around the table halted their conversations, and looked her way.

Lifting her glass high, Joi continued. "To the women of Citadel. Protecting the business assets of this city isn't easy, but we're just the right women for the job."

"Here, here." An assortment of goblets and glasses were raised in salute.

Sitting back down, Joi felt Karen jab her in the ribs with her elbow.

"Why didn't you give my toast?" Karen's mock pout was pronounced.

"No, Karen. If you want to give it go ahead, but I'm the boss and I'm not about to say that."

Rolling her eyes playfully, Karen backed off.

Kim, a Marine veteran and the elder stateswoman of Citadel's guard staff, raised her glass. "I'll do it, Karen. Here's to those who wish us well. And those who don't, can go to hell."

The women around the table broke out in peals of laughter. Mindful of her role as the owner and guard supervisor, Joi contained her mirth. Still, she couldn't stop the smile from spreading across her face at the snarky declaration.

"I'm just glad we were able to get the contract." The comment came from Carol, a thirtysomething mother of two who was formerly one of Charlotte's finest. "I enjoyed my time walking my beat, but I'm not trying to go back to the force. Not at my age."

"I feel you." Joi knew that even on her easiest day on the police force, Carol's old job was never as relaxed as her current post, guarding the patrons and assets of a ritzy dog salon in midtown Charlotte. Along with Carol, both Maxine and Traci, two of the other guards on Citadel's staff, came from police backgrounds.

Rose, swallowing a bite of her food, chimed in. "I agree. I'm way past the age of going back on deck. I've been on land so long I'm sure I've lost my sea legs. Right, Sheryl?"

Sheryl nodded, but chose not to speak around a

mouthful of food. Both she and Rose had served in the US Navy.

Yolanda and Jackie, the two guards who'd been displaced from their positions when Mrs. Clark's boutique had shut down, were both Army vets. Joi felt the two of them were particularly suited to the bank contract, since they were both taller and more muscular in build. Of all the places Citadel had a security presence, Joi was sure the bank was the place where physical prowess was most likely to become necessary.

Yolanda, scrolling through something on her phone, quipped, "I'm looking forward to handling the bank job. I just know some young buck is gonna try to break bad with me."

Jackie snickered. "You're always looking for a fight."

Yolanda shook her head. "Not really. I just won't back down from one."

Joi shook her head, as well. She was used to that type of banter between the two of them. Yolanda could be a bit of a hothead, but she was also a professional. Aside from that, Jackie's cool and collected nature provided the perfect balance that made the two of them such a great team.

Joi scooted her hips over the leather seat of the booth's bench, bumping into Karen. "Let me out." All the iced tea she'd been drinking was now looking for a new home.

Karen stood, allowing Joi to scoot out of the booth.

On her feet now, Joi told the rest of the girls, "I'll be back." Then she turned and went off in search of the ladies' room.

Within a few minutes, she'd handled her needs,

washed up and checked her reflection. As she left the ladies' room, heading back for her booth, she saw a dark-haired man in a suit coming toward her.

That can't be who I think it is.

Most of the light in the place was coming from the recessed lighting in the ceiling, which made it hard to see clearly. She slowed her steps as she came closer to the man.

His steps did not slow.

By the time she realized it really was Marco Alvarez strolling her way, he'd already entered her personal space.

"Ah, Ms. Lewis. It is you." His hand was gripped around the handles of a large plastic bag bearing the restaurant's logo.

"Hello, Mr. Alvarez. My team and I were just enjoying a meal together. We have a very good rapport with one another." She drummed her fingertips against her thigh.

"I gather that, based on all the noise coming from your table."

Her eyebrow hitched. Just how long had he been there? And why in the hell had he been listening in on their conversation? She had many questions, but she knew better than to ask them. "I hope we aren't the reason you're taking your meal to go." She gestured to his bag.

He shook his head, a half smile on his face. "No. I always get my food to go here. I don't care for the atmosphere half as much as I do the ribs."

"I see." She moved to his right, hoping to walk around him and put an end to their awkward conversation. But before she could make two good steps, he cleared his throat.

Sensing he was trying to get her attention, she stopped walking, and turned back in his direction. "Yes, Mr. Alvarez?"

The half smile remained on his handsome, burnished face. "You can call me Marco, you know."

As she viewed the appealing shagginess of his slight five o'clock shadow, she shook her head. "I think it's better if we keep things professional between us, Mr. Alvarez." She emphasized the title and his last name.

He scratched his chin with his free hand, as if thinking about something. "No one else who works in the bank calls me Mr. Alvarez."

Now it was her turn to smile. "I assure you, Mr. Alvarez, I'm not like anyone who works in your bank."

And with that, she turned on her heel and started walking back toward her table.

Watching Joi's back as she walked away, Marco felt his brow furrow. Had she just dismissed him? He was pretty sure she had, because he hadn't had a chance to say what was on his mind. He was also pretty sure that he didn't like her walking away from him that way. If their business relationship was going to work out, she needed to know that.

With the bag containing his rapidly cooling food in his hand, he strolled across the dining room, in the direction he'd seen her retreat. When he located the corner booth where she was sitting, he stopped beside it.

Letting the bevy of women see his most dazzling smile, he announced his presence. "Good evening, ladies. Are you enjoying yourselves?"

A bumper crop of smiles, cooed greetings and appreciative glances were flung his way, which only served to brighten his smile. Women had been responding to him this way since he was a boy of ten, and tonight was no exception.

He noted that, once again, Joi seemed immune to his charms. She was the only woman at the table whose face didn't appear welcoming. While her friends were basically batting their eyelashes at him, Joi looked like she was sucking a lemon.

Finally, she announced, "Ladies, this is Marco Alvarez."

That seemed to sober the atmosphere at the table, because all of the women dialed back their overt flirting right away. He wondered what Joi had said to them about him.

Speaking again, he asked, "Would you mind if I stole Ms. Lewis for a moment?"

All eyes at the table turned to Joi. He could see her squirming under the scrutiny, and he also saw the rosy color rising into her cheeks.

Her expression remained flat and unreadable as she said, "Sure, Mr. Alvarez."

The woman beside Joi allowed her out of the booth, and once she was on her feet, Marco made a sweeping gesture. "We can step outside. I promise this won't take long."

She said nothing, but walked past him in the direction of the door.

He took in her attire as he moved behind her. She'd changed from the business suit he'd seen her in at their eventful interview. Now, she wore a figure-hugging sweater dress, in a soft orange color that complemented

her skin tone beautifully. The dress reached her ankles, and had long sleeves, but there was no denying
the shapely body beneath the garment. Walking behind
her made it fairly difficult to avoid staring at her der-
riere, but he raised his gaze nonetheless.

Once they were both outside the glass doors of the
restaurant, sheltered beneath a black-and-gold awning,
she stopped and turned to him. "What is this about,
Mr. Alvarez?"

Unable to hold the words back, he spoke. "You look
very nice tonight, Ms. Lewis."

She folded her arms across her chest, but kept her
expression unreadable. "Thank you, but I hope you
didn't ask me to come out here just to tell me that."

He wanted to scoff, but refrained. He sensed that
would only make their interactions more unpleasant.
"No. This is about the two of us."

One of her neatly shaped brows rose.

He realized she might be getting the wrong impression, so he sought to clarify his statement. "If we're
going to have a good working relationship, I'll need
to know I can trust you."

She shifted her weight, and dropped her arms. "I
come highly recommended, and I have an impeccable
record of getting the job done for my clients."

"I know that. But we're going to have to address
our past history, Joi. I'm going to want an explanation
of what happened between you and…"

She put up her hand. "I'd rather not hear his name.
And that is a personal matter between him and me,
not something that should be brought up between us."

"So you're not going to address it at all?"

She shrugged. "There's nothing to address. What happened six years ago has no bearing on my ability to perform the job you've contracted me for. Are we done here?"

He could see her gaze was focused on the restaurant door. Since she wasn't going to tell him anything, he didn't see any good reason to hold her up. "Yes, Ms. Lewis. I'll see you Tuesday. I like to get my guards acclimated for the first couple of weeks before I step back and let them do their job."

"Thank you." As the curt response left her lips, she strode past him, and disappeared into the restaurant.

For a few moments, he stood in her wake. Then he took his probably cold food to his car, climbed in and started the engine.

As he drove through the streets of midtown Charlotte, he engaged his car's hands-free calling functionality to call his mother.

When her voice came over the speaker, he smiled. "*Feliz cumpleonos*, Mama."

Her response was tinged with delight. "Thank you, Marco. You are such a good son. You never forget your Mama's birthday, no matter how busy you are."

He chuckled. Today had been a hectic one, but he would never forget a day so special. "Of course not. Did you get the flowers I sent you?"

"Yes, and thank you for those, too. They are gorgeous. But don't you think you went a little overboard? They must have been very expensive."

"No price is too high for you, Mama." Sure, sending sixty-five yellow roses to his mother, all the way back home in Costa Rica, had been costly. But since he couldn't be there in person, he'd thought it appropriate to send her the flowers in her favorite color, with one bloom for each year she'd graced the earth with her presence.

"You're such a dear, but you know I hate being fussed over."

He shook his head, knowing the exact opposite to be true. "Enjoy them, Mama."

"I am, but don't spend so much next time. You already work much too hard, and I don't want you going into debt on frivolity."

"Yes, Mama." He knew that was the only response she would accept.

"You know what I really want for my birthday, or for any day, for that matter."

He sighed. He'd known this was coming, but he'd hoped the grand gesture of the flowers would distract her from it. "Yes, Mama. I know. You want grandchildren."

"At this point, I would settle for a grandchild, singular. When are you going to settle down and bring me some babies to spoil?"

Keeping his eyes on the road, even as his mind searched for the proper response, he swung his car into his driveway. "Mama, when the time is right, I will settle down. You have my word."

With love in her voice, she said, "I only want happiness for you, my dear."

"I know, Mama. I love you, and I'll call you again in a few days. Give my best to Papa."

"I love you, as well."

He ended the call just as he pulled into his garage. A few moments later, he cut the engine. Grabbing the bag from the passenger seat, he took his food inside the house.

The echoes of his mother's words dogged him at each step.

Chapter 4

"Something doesn't look right." Joi tilted her head slightly to the right, trying to look at her painting from a different angle. But no matter how she stared, it still bore little resemblance to the potted white orchid she was supposed to be re-creating.

She was sitting on a low stool at Wine and Whimsy, taking their Saturday-evening class. The wine and paint shop, owned by her older sister, Joanne, was her favorite weekend hangout. While she didn't think she had any talent for painting at all, she recognized the stress-relieving power of creativity.

Joanne, clad in her bright blue apron, eased over to where she sat. "Complaining about your painting again? I could hear you grousing on the other side of the room."

Adding another stroke of white paint to one of her

misshapen petals, Joi blew out a breath. "Mine doesn't look anything like the display. I suck at this."

The woman next to her, who was about halfway into her second glass of merlot, said, "It looks pretty good to me. Maybe you just haven't had enough wine."

Joanne chuckled. "Loretta's right, in a way. Relax, and stop being such a perfectionist. Art is all about interpretation, and self-expression."

Joi looked from her sister to the painting and back again. "Well, that must mean I interpret this flower to be crooked, and I'm expressing it that way."

"Whatever, girl. I'm going to help somebody who's actually paying for this." With a shake of her head, Joanne moved on to converse with another "budding artist."

Watching her sister waft around the room like a cool breeze, Joi smiled. Growing up, the two of them had occupied very specific roles in their household. Joanne, three years older than Joi, had been the tall, graceful sister with a talent for the arts. Joi had been the shorter, more awkward tomboy, who'd excelled in sports. Both of them had performed well academically, but while Joi pursued her criminal justice degree at North Carolina Central University, Joanne had gotten her bachelor of fine arts from the Art Institute of Atlanta. Following in the footsteps of their mother, Emma, a seamstress who owned a small clothing boutique, both Joanne and Joi had gone on to find fulfillment and success in entrepreneurship.

After spending the remainder of the class trying to even out the crooked petals of her painted orchid, Joi threw in the towel and put down her brush. Her hands and the blue smock she wore were stained with paint, as was the plastic wineglass she'd been drinking rosé from. Narrowing her eyes at the painting, she had to agree with Loretta. Now that she had a full glass of wine in her system, her painting did look a whole lot better.

Once the other women had emptied out of the shop, Joanne returned to her side. "Are you ready to hang it yet? Because I'm technically closed, and I would like to go home sometime tonight."

Lifting the painting from the easel, Joi handed it over to her sister. "Yep. But hang it in the back, by your office."

Joanne accepted the canvas, and Joi looked on as she took it to the short hallway that led to her office, the break room and the restrooms of the shop. Once the painting was hung, she returned. "It will only be there for a few days, until it dries. You can come pick it up then."

Joi nodded. "I will. I'm not sure I want you to keep it on permanent display."

Folding her arms across her chest, Joanne narrowed her eyes. "Joi, what's up with you?"

Feeling a little uncomfortable under her older sister's knowing gaze, she started cleaning up her paint station. "What do you mean?"

"Girl, please. You've got something on your mind, and we both know it, so you might as well spill it."

With a sigh, Joi tucked her brushes into the well of cleaning solution. "Remember I told you I won that bank contract for Citadel?"

"Yeah, what about it?"

"Well, what I didn't tell you is that Marco Alvarez is the bank president, so technically, I'll be working for him."

Joanne's brow creased at the mention of Marco's name. "Marco. Marco. The name sounds familiar, but where do you know him from?"

Sliding the stool under the table, Joi said, "He was Ernesto's best man."

Surprise widened Joanne's eyes. "Oh."

"Oh is right."

"I'm guessing he wants some answers about what happened back then." Joanne grabbed a cloth and began wiping down the ten paint stations scattered around the main room.

"Yes. As a matter of fact, I ran into him at Mimosa Grill last night, and he brought it up."

"What did you tell him?"

"Nothing, except that what happened between Ernesto and I is a personal matter that has nothing to do with my work."

"Hmm." Joanne probably had something else to say on the matter, but she kept it to herself.

"I don't know if he'll bring it up again, or what I'll say if he does. And if that's not bad enough…" Joi let her voice trail off as she picked up a second cloth to help her sister with the closing duties.

"What? What aren't you saying?"

"I…well…I kind of like him."

Joanne stopped scrubbing, turning wide eyes on her baby sister. "Joi, are you trying to tell me you're attracted to him?"

"He's fine, Joanne. I mean, he was good-looking back in the day, but now he's completely, totally, utterly, five-alarm smoking *hot*."

Still staring, Joanne stammered, "But he's your ex-fiancé's friend, Joi. And he's about to be your boss! Ain't nobody that damn hot."

"I beg to differ." Joi pulled out her smartphone, and did a quick internet image search. When she found Marco's photo on the bank's website, she sidled over to where her sister stood furiously scrubbing a blob of red paint off the tabletop and showed it to her. "Look at him."

Joanne's eyes rounded even more, and her bottom jaw dropped so fast and far, Joi though it might hit the floor.

"Well?" Joi waited.

"Damn." Joanne's one-word response was half sighed, half spoken.

A vindicated Joi tucked the phone back into the hip pocket of her jeans. "Like I said, five-alarm hotness."

Joanne, staring ahead into space as if she could still see Marco's photo, had a look of amazement on her face. "He has that whole tall, dark and handsome thing going on. But he took it to the max." After a few seconds, she seemed to snap out of it, and went back to scrubbing.

"I told you. How do you think I felt when I walked into his office for my appointment? It was all I could do not to drool on his desk during my proposal."

Joanne, having finally removed the stubborn paint stain, tossed her cloth back into the bucket and shook her head slowly. "Congrats on containing your drool, I know that wasn't easy. But you do know that if you start something up with him, you'll be asking for trouble, right?"

"I never said I was going to start anything with him, I just pointed out how fine he was."

Joanne hit her with a side-eyed glance. "Girl, please. If you're standing here telling me all this, you're thinking about it. Not that I blame you. That man is finer than frog's hair."

Joi made a fist and punched her sister in the shoulder. "Stop teasing me, Jo."

Feigning injury from the playful blow, Joanne grimaced. "All kidding aside, be careful, Joi. I don't want to see you get hurt, nor do I want to see your business go down in flames, all because you couldn't resist getting busy with the Casanova banker here."

Joi, shrugging into her coat, smacked her lips. "I'm not planning on anything like that happening, Joanne. I can't just think about myself. I've got a business partner and several employees to consider, so I can't afford to be frivolous."

"I just hope you remember that the next time you're alone in a room with Marco." Joanne tightened the belt on her own coat.

"I will." Even as Joi spoke the words, she wondered if she could really deny the intense attraction sparking between her and Marco, or if she even wanted to.

"Let's go. I want to get home before too late, so I can look in on Marlon." Joanne smiled as she spoke of her six-year-old son with her husband, Victor.

"Cool. I wouldn't dream of keeping my nephew from his mommy." Joi walked toward the door her sister held open for her, and after Joanne locked up, the two of them got into Joanne's minivan and departed.

His eyes settled on the big-screen television displaying the Carolina-Atlanta football game, and Marco popped a cheese fry into his mouth. The open window blinds at the Brash Bull allowed the deceptively bright sunlight to stream into the sports bar's interior, casting thin beams of light on the concrete floor. Glancing out that window might make one think it was warm outside, but Marco knew better. He'd ventured out into the biting chill of this mid-November Sunday. If it weren't for his affection for football and the company of his friends, he would have stayed home. Again he wondered if he'd ever get used to the chill that hung in the air this time of year, making him long for the balmy shores of his home back in Limón.

Seated around the table with him were his three friends and bandmates, Darius, Rashad and Ken. Together, the four of them were the jazz quartet known as the Queen City Gents. Darius, retired and wealthy at thirty-seven thanks to his tech-savvy invention, played the upright bass. Rashad, a museum curator, sang lead vocals and played piano. And Ken, an architect originally from Japan, acted as the quartet's drummer. Marco's tenor saxophone rounded out the group. He liked to think his skills on the golden horn added a special depth and richness to the Gents' music.

Rashad, who had recently returned from his honeymoon in Trinidad and Tobago with his new wife, Lina, pounded his fist on the table. "Damn. We've got more turnovers today than a bakery."

Marco chuckled, his friend was right. Cheering for Carolina could sometimes be difficult, but the four of them weren't fair-weather or bandwagon fans. "Don't worry. Remember, we really come alive in the second half."

Darius, draining the last of the root beer in his mug, groused, "Yeah, but we need to start playing all four quarters. This is bad for my nerves."

Ken, looking up from the screen of his tablet, snorted a laugh. "Statistically, the odds are in Carolina's favor. So don't sweat it."

Marco shook his head. They all knew that Ken never got very excited about anything, hence his nickname, "Ken the Zen."

Washing down his buffalo wings with a swig of lemonade, Rashad smiled. "Even if we lose, knowing I get to go home to Lina makes everything all right."

That comment split the group into two factions: the married men, and the single ones. Marco and Ken both offered groans, as if offended by Rashad's sentimental observation.

Darius gave Rashad a hard slap on the back as he nodded in agreement. "Amen to that, man. Nothing like the love of a good woman." He shared a knowing grin with Rashad, as if they were members of some kind of secret club.

With a roll of his eyes, Marco remarked, "You two are so whipped. A year ago neither of you were even interested in a relationship. Now suddenly you're the poster boys for upstanding husbands?"

"Stop hating, Marco. You know you want what we have." Darius cut him with a hard stare.

"Why would I want to give up my freedom?"

Rashad shook his head. "I used to think I was giving up something, and I guess, in a way, I did. But what I gained is worth so much more."

"Right. My life is a thousand times better now that I have Eve in my life." Darius leaned back in his chair, a wistful look on his face. "And with the baby coming, my life is really going to be complete."

"Wow. You two are really drinking the marriage

Kool-Aid." Marco looked across the table at the men, his closest friends. The grins Darius and Rashad wore spoke to their happiness, but it was still difficult for him to wrap his mind around it.

Their transformation from single guys to family men was something he still hadn't gotten used to. Deep down, he supposed they were still the same guys he'd met all those years ago, when he'd first showed up at rehearsal to answer their ad for a saxophonist. Still, the sappy nature of their recent conversations had begun to stick in his craw.

"Whatever. I know it was the best decision I ever made." Rashad redirected his attention toward the television, now showing the halftime show.

Marco stuffed another cheese fry into his mouth. He would never admit it aloud, but he felt a twinge of jealousy at his friends' declarations of bliss. Who wouldn't? They made marriage sound like the best thing since the invention of twenty-four-hour sports coverage. He'd had his share of experience with marriage, from watching his parents. They'd been married more than forty years, so he knew true love wasn't a myth. He also knew that with love and marriage came children, bills and more responsibility than he ever wanted to have. No, he wasn't marriage material, but then again, not everybody was meant for marital bliss. "I can have any woman I want, so why should I settle for just one? Am I right, Ken?" Marco dug his elbow into Ken's forearm.

Ken, seated to Marco's right, glanced up from the glowing screen of his tablet, a confused look on his face. "Sorry, what did you say?"

Marco scoffed. "Thanks for the backup, man."

"You're welcome." With a shrug, Ken dropped his eyes back to the screen, and kept right on scrolling.

As the halftime show ended and coverage returned to the game, silence fell over the table. Marco felt a modicum of relief. While he didn't begrudge his friends living their lives as they saw fit, all that stuff about wives and babies really put a damper on the whole male bonding thing.

The rest of the game went by with only conversation surrounding cheering for the home team to crush the visiting squad. In the end, Carolina won out by three points, thanks to the kicker's flawless field goal attempt. That got everybody at the table on their feet, laughing and exchanging high fives.

While the waitress cleared the table of their empty plates and mugs, Darius spoke up. "Oh yeah, guys, I almost forgot. I got a call from Dave, and it looks like we're in for the Winter Jazz Festival."

Marco's ears perked up at that. "Awesome! Who are we opening for? Who are we following?"

Ken, having finally tucked his tablet away, asked, "What are we making on this gig?"

Darius snorted a laugh, shaking his head. "All right, Gents, one question at a time. We're going on before Mint Condition, and following Eric Jackson. So step your game up, sax man." He looked at Marco and gave him a playful thump on the forehead.

Marco thumped him back. "My sax game is always on point."

Rashad, leaning against the short dividing wall behind their table, chimed in. "I'm with Ken. I wanna know how much we're getting paid. Lina's got expensive tastes." He chuckled at his own joke.

"The deal is four grand up front, plus two percent of the ticket sales. In other words, if we advertise the festival every week at our shows, we can raise our take." Darius fished his phone out of his pocket and looked at the screen. "The festival is the second weekend of December, so keep your calendars clear."

Ken remarked, "Us? Isn't your wife due around that time?"

Darius nodded. "She's due at the end of this month, and if she's late, they'll induce her."

Rashad snickered. "Based on what Lina's been telling me, Eve's miserable. Trust me, she ain't holding that kid in any longer than necessary."

"Quit teasing my wife. You'll be there soon enough." Darius gave Rashad a fake punch in the shoulder.

Marco laughed to himself at their horseplay. Yeah, they were definitely the same dudes he'd grown to know and...tolerate. "Sounds good. Even if we don't do anything to help them sell tickets, we should still make a decent amount of cash on top of the up-front money. What are we doing with it this time?"

Darius gestured to Ken, who was shrugging into his dark brown trench coat. "It's Ken's turn to pick."

Ken, busy patting his pockets in search of something, replied, "Children's Miracle Network."

Marco nodded his approval. "Good deal, man. By the way, your keys are on the table."

Ceasing the fruitless patting, Ken finally spotted the keys among the pile of crumpled napkins on the tabletop, and picked them up. "Thanks."

Each time the Gents performed at a paid gig, they donated half the money to a charity and split the difference. Since the four of them were all pretty well set financially, they'd all agreed to put that portion of their earnings toward helping causes they supported. In the past, they'd donated to veterans' charities, homeless shelters and organizations that provided services to battered women.

As the men exchanged goodbyes and left the Brash Bull, Marco thought about the coming week, and everything it would hold. Most of his concern centered on Joi, and the attraction buzzing between them like an electric current. He wasn't fully sure he could trust her, yet he couldn't stop himself from admiring the woman she'd become. Shaking his head, he unlocked his car door and climbed inside the cabin.

Chapter 5

Joi had never been one to slack on any job she'd been entrusted with. That's why when Marco and Roosevelt arrived on Tuesday morning to unlock the doors of the bank branch, Joi and her team were already there.

It was another chilly day, and she'd draped her heavy houndstooth jacket over her uniform to protect her from the cool air. She sat on the old wooden bench in front of the building housing Royal Bank and Trust with one leg crossed casually over the other. Next to Joi sat her partner, Karen, as well as Yolanda and Jackie, the two guards she'd assigned to the job.

A smirk touched Joi's lips as she took in the shocked expressions of the two men. "Good morning, gentlemen."

Roosevelt offered a nod and a grunt in response. Joi quickly gathered that the older man wasn't a fan of early mornings.

Marco, with the large ring of keys in hand, returned her smile. "Good morning, ladies. I see you're here bright and early."

Joi stood, and the rest of her staff followed suit. "That's the Citadel way. Show up early, stay late, get the job done right."

His facial expression changed, revealing that he was impressed. "I like that attitude. Give me a few moments and we can all go inside out of this cold."

Karen and the guards formed an orderly line behind Joi, and waited while Marco fit the key into the lock. He then swung the door open, and Joi led her team into the heated interior of the bank building.

Relieved to be inside, Joi led Karen and their guards as she followed Roosevelt to the employee break room. There, everyone hung their coats in the small closet, before reporting back to the main lobby area.

Joi looked around for Marco, but didn't see him. Assuming he'd already disappeared into his office for the day, she focused on getting her team prepared for their first day on the job. This was a lucrative contract, and she aimed to show Marco, as well as the bankers he reported to, that Citadel was very capable of serving all of their security needs.

When the four of them were all seated in chairs in the waiting area, Joi began her daily briefing. "Ladies, this is our first day at Royal, and we want to make it as smooth as possible."

"I'm ready to start the cybersecurity hardware and software setup, but my assistant won't be here until nine." Karen slipped her hands out of her gloves and tucked them into her purse.

"Fine. Just do what you can until she comes in." Joi

snapped her fingers, remembering the small boxes in her blazer pocket. Extracting two, she extended them toward her guards. "I almost forgot. These are for Veterans Day. Thank you for your service, ladies."

Each woman took a box. Yolanda opened hers to reveal a silver charm bracelet filled with patriotic charms. "Thank you, Joi. It's lovely."

A smile touched Joi's lips. "It's the least I can do. My grandfather was an Army vet. He served at Normandy during World War II." She'd gone to the cemetery yesterday to place a bouquet of red, white and blue flowers on James Lewis's grave, but decided not to mention that, in order to keep the conversation light.

Once Yolanda and Jackie had tucked their bracelets away, Joi proceeded with the briefing.

"Jackie, I'm assigning you to the vault and the periphery around the offices. Yolanda, you'll be patrolling the lobby and the parking lot. We have about half an hour before the bank opens, so spend that time familiarizing yourself with the layout. Did you all look over the maps I gave you?"

Everyone indicated that they had.

Joi spent a few more moments explaining the day's tasks to her guards, then sent them to their posts. Karen had already disappeared into the branch manager's office, so Joi left the lobby in search of Marco.

She stopped in front of his office door, which was slightly ajar. She glanced inside the room and saw him sitting at his desk, poring over a stack of paperwork.

She raised her fist to rap on the door, but before she could, his head jerked up.

His eyes locked with hers, he gave her an assessing look. "Ms. Lewis. Come in, please. I'd like to talk with you."

She eased the door open and stepped inside his office. Just as it had been the last time she'd come here, she felt overwhelmed by the masculine presence in the room. The decor, with its dark paint, wood paneling and hulking desk, seemed to be a reflection of the virility and power exuded by the man who occupied the space.

"I'm impressed with you and your staff being so early this morning, but that really won't be necessary in the future." He leaned forward in his chair, resting his elbows on the desk.

"Whatever you think is best, Mr. Alvarez."

"So, is there no way I can get you to call me Marco? Or have you forgotten my request that you address me by my first name?"

She shook her head, because she clearly remembered his request. She also clearly remembered the heady feeling he aroused in her, and she knew getting too informal with him would be a bad idea. "I remember, I'm just not comfortable with it. At least not yet."

He tented his fingers. "Fair enough. We'll revisit it another time. But there is something I need to ask you. It may sound personal, but it's really not."

She could feel her brow furrow, and the tension rising up her spine. "What more do you want to know?"

"More than the stiff response you gave me before. What have you been doing these last six years? You seem very different from the woman I remember."

She felt her shoulders tense. From the way he'd made the statement, she couldn't tell whether he thought the current version of her was an improvement. Pushing that thought aside, she answered his question. "Let's see. I was fresh out of college. Since then, I've studied martial arts, gotten my black belt in Tae Kwon Do, became certified in self-defense and, oh, got a cat."

His brow hitched at the last part. "A cat?"

"Yep. She's all gray and her name is Misty." In reality, she didn't have a pet, but if telling him that would satisfy his nosiness, so be it.

A slight smile turned up the corners of his mouth, brightening his otherwise stern countenance.

For a moment, she smiled back, thinking she'd succeeded in getting him to lighten up. Her hopes were dashed when he spoke again.

"So, have you dated much?" He fixed her with a penetrating, almost accusatory stare.

Gazing back into the pools of his dark eyes, she sighed. "No, I haven't. Not that that's any of your business."

"That's true, it's not my business."

She stared at him, wondering what he was playing at. "Then why did you ask? And what does that have to do with anything?"

He ran his fingertips over his chin. "I'm trying to establish trust. But I don't know if we can ever have that as long as you refuse to talk about Ernesto."

She closed her eyes, so he wouldn't see her rolling them. "This again? I already told you, I don't want to address it."

He leaned back in his chair, and kept his gaze steady. "Eventually, you'll have to tell me why you ran, Joi."

She folded her arms over her chest. "Well, today isn't the day."

She knew that if she remained in his office, they

might end up arguing. As she'd told Joanne, she had her entire staff to think about, and Citadel needed the Royal Bank contract. So to avoid getting into a conflict with him that might jeopardize her company's future, she turned and strode out of the office.

As she made her way through the corridor toward the lobby, she wondered how she could possibly be attracted to a man who was so contentious and stubborn.

Darkly handsome or not, Marco Alvarez was trouble, and Joi knew she had to keep things strictly professional between them, no matter how hard that might be.

The last customer of the day left the bank around fifteen minutes before closing time. Once he knew the closing duties had been completed, Marco let Roosevelt and his three tellers go home for the day. Citadel's guards departed right after the bank staff.

As he made his rounds of the bank's interior in preparation to leave, his thoughts swung to Joi. He hadn't seen her since she'd stalked out of his office earlier, and he assumed she might have left for the day. She'd made it clear she hadn't liked his line of questioning, and had spent the rest of the day avoiding him.

From what he gathered, Joi would be present at the bank for at least the first two weeks, to get her guards adjusted to their new position. Joi's partner, who was apparently the tech guru, had yet to make an appearance. He had no indication she ever would.

As he turned the corner of the corridor near the vault and his office, he spotted Joi. She was seated in one of the chairs in the waiting area, with a pair of earbud headphones in her ears. She didn't seem to notice him, as her full attention was on writing something on the metal clipboard that lay across her lap.

He took a step back and watched her for a moment. Despite her stubborn streak and her outer bravado, Joi Lewis was a stunning woman. Her uniform, crisply pressed and professional in every way, still did little to hide the womanly curves of her body. He observed her demure posture, with one of her legs crossed over the other, and the graceful way her hand moved the pen over the surface of the paper. Her brow furrowed ever so slightly. Her pouty lips were pursed. She appeared to be in deep concentration, and he didn't want to intrude on whatever she was working on. So he leaned his shoulder against the wall, content to enjoy the view for as long as he could.

She stopped writing and inclined her head. "Mr. Alvarez?"

Knowing he was caught, Marco stepped into the lobby and walked closer to where she sat. "We're the only two people left in the building. Are you ready to go?"

She popped out one of her earbuds. "I'm sorry, what did you say?"

He repeated, "Are you ready to go?"

"Yes. Just finished up the day's reports." She shuffled through her papers, then opened the lid of her clipboard and slipped them inside.

The familiar sound of the music flowing from her headphones caught Marco's attention. He listened for a couple of seconds, then began to hum along. "You're listening to Coltrane?"

She nodded. "*Lush Life*. It's my favorite Coltrane album."

Grooving to the sounds of the third track, "Trane's Slo Blues," Marco tapped his foot in time. "That's a sign of great taste. If you're a Coltrane fan, I think we can get along just fine."

She offered him a slight smile. "I think we can get along great, as long as you stay out of my personal business."

He grimaced, as if stung. "Wow. I walked right into that one, didn't I?"

"You sure did." She chuckled, removing the other earbud. After taking a few moments to turn off the music program on her phone, she tucked it and the headphones away in her purse.

When she stood, his eyes swept over her form again, lingering at the round lines of her hips.

"Mr. Alvarez, my face is up here." Her censuring tone grabbed his attention.

Swinging his gaze back toward her face, he smiled. "Forgive my lack of manners, Ms. Lewis."

She said nothing, but her expression seemed to convey disapproval. She gathered her purse and clipboard, went to stand by the main entrance. As he approached, keys in hand, he reached out to push the door open.

Joi reached out at the same moment, and his hand landed atop hers on the pressure bar.

The moment their fingers touched, he felt a tingle run through his body. She must've felt it as well, because she startled and drew her hand back within a few seconds. The door, which had only just separated from the seal, clicked back into a closed position.

When he turned to look at her, he could see the heat in her cheeks.

In that moment, he knew he had to address the attraction crackling between them. If he didn't speak up, there was no way they'd be able to work together every day. Before he could get his speech off the ground though, she spoke.

"Mr. Alvarez, I think it's better if we address this now."

His brow hitched. "You mean the attraction between us?"

She nodded, her gaze drifting up to meet his. "You're a handsome man, and I would be lying if I said I wasn't attracted to you."

He couldn't stop the smile curling his lips. "I won't deny how I feel about you, either."

"And how is that?"

"Like a schoolboy with a crush." It was an honest answer, and the best way he could think of to describe the way he felt whenever she entered his space.

She moved in, closing the space between them. A sly smile graced her full lips. "Oh, really?"

"Really." He raised his hand, letting his knuckle graze the soft skin of her jaw. She trembled, but didn't back away or reject his touch.

A moment later he dipped his head and placed a pensive kiss on her jaw. She quickly turned her head, and their lips met.

He let the kiss deepen naturally, reveling in the softness of her lips. She laid one hand on his shoulder, and let the other cup his jaw, as the tip of her tongue grazed against his.

He felt himself leaning backward as she pressed her body closer to his. Their combined weight depressed the pressure bar, and the door swung open, letting a blast of cold air into the space.

She broke the kiss, and he grabbed the door frame to steady them both as the door opened fully. When he looked at her again, he could see the conflicted expression playing across her features.

Her brown eyes filled with something unreadable. She then whispered, "What the hell did we just do?"

Now that she'd put her doubts into words, he searched for the right thing to say, something to put her at ease again. "You're a beautiful woman, Joi Lewis. And I see no reason why we can't enjoy each other's company."

She shook her head. "I do. I want to win this contract on merit, not because we're involved. That isn't the way I do business." She edged past him and started to walk away.

He let the door swing shut and went after her, laying his hand on her arm just as she stepped off the curb. "Wait. Let's talk about this."

"There's nothing to talk about." She glanced at the silver wristwatch she wore. "I'm late for an appointment with another client. I really have to go."

He released her, and she strode across the parking lot to her pickup truck.

He cursed under his breath as he watched her climb into the truck and drive away into the night. By giving in to his inexplicable desire for her, he'd succeeded in making things even more awkward between them. Lamenting how royally he'd screwed up by kissing her, he went back to secure the bank.

Chapter 6

Joi angrily swiped her finger across the screen of her smartphone Wednesday morning, to cease the shrill ringing of her alarm. Once the sound stopped, she yawned and rubbed her bleary eyes. She sat up and scooted to the edge of the bed and swung her legs over the side, seeking the furry warmth of her slippers. After sliding her feet into them, she shuffled across her room to the bathroom, all the while wondering how she was supposed to face this day on so little sleep.

After she'd gone through the rigors of her morning grooming ritual, she slipped into a clean uniform. The hot shower had left her feeling refreshed and a bit more awake, but coffee would have to finish the job.

While her cup of joe brewed, she thought back on the previous day and her encounter with Marco. Her fingertips grazed over her lips as she remembered the wicked warmth of his kiss, and the way he'd made her melt into her shoes like butter in a hot skillet. She shook her head at the memory. Thinking about his skillful lips was the very reason she'd lain awake most of the night.

He'd kissed her, and she hadn't stopped him. She hadn't even hesitated, and if she were honest with herself, she had to admit that she'd enjoyed it. Kissing Marco hadn't felt like any other kiss she'd ever shared with a man, and as far as she was concerned, that spelled trouble. She'd shown up late for her appointment last night at Le Petit Chien, a ritzy midtown boutique where Carol, one of her guards, was assigned. She'd had to fix her hair and makeup in the car before going in, to keep Penny, the chatty spa owner, from seeing her looking disheveled and out of sorts.

The smell of the freshly brewed French roast filled her kitchen, drawing her out of her thoughts. She went to retrieve the travel mug she'd placed beneath the dispenser and lifted it to her nose, deeply inhaling the earthy fragrance. After doctoring the coffee up with a hint of cream and sugar, she grabbed a protein bar, her purse and her clipboard, and headed outside to her truck.

All the way to the bank, she continued to entertain thoughts of Marco while she sipped from the mug of life-giving brew. She anticipated things being very weird between the two of them today, and she didn't want to complicate things any further than their bad judgment already had. So by the time she parked her truck in the bank's lot, she'd made up her mind to go straight to him and tell him that their first kiss would also be their last.

She arrived a few minutes after the bank's opening time, so the doors were open and she was sure staff members were already inside. She walked into the bank, resolute in her decision. As she strode through the lobby toward Marco's office, she offered greetings to the two tellers, to Roosevelt and to Yolanda. When she reached the office, she saw the door standing partially open. Despite that, she erred on the side of caution and gave the surface of the door a few light raps.

He appeared in the doorway. "Come on in, Ms. Lewis."

She did as he asked, easing into the office and closing the door behind her. He'd taken a few steps back to allow her entry.

Unfortunately, he didn't step back far enough, because her chest briefly made contact with his. She jerked her body to the right, in an effort to put space between them. She succeeded, but nearly toppled over in the process.

His strong arm swung out in a flash, steadying her moments before she went crashing to the floor.

"Are you all right?" His voice and his eyes both held concern.

She straightened, tugged the strap of her purse to bring it back up on her shoulder. Knowing better than to tell him how his touch made her feel, she said, "Yes, I'm fine. Thank you."

Apparently he sensed her discomfort, because he moved his arm and stepped back. "No problem."

Taking a deep breath, she wished she could hit Rewind and repeat her entrance. Since that wasn't an option, she put on her most pleasant expression. "Good morning, Mr. Alvarez."

Casually perching on the edge of the desktop near

where she stood, he offered her a slight smile. "Good morning, Ms. Lewis. I see we're still being formal with each other."

She closed her eyes momentarily, hoping that if she couldn't see his dark handsomeness, it might be easier for her to say what she'd come to say. "Yes. I won't take up too much of your time…"

"I'm in no hurry." His deep voice filled her ears, and he didn't bother masking the invitation in his tone.

She opened her eyes and cleared her throat. Avoiding looking directly at him, she stated, "I just wanted to apologize for letting myself get carried away yesterday evening."

"I assume you're referring to our kiss?" One of his thick brows lifted, as if he were amused.

She nodded, her gaze lowering. She busied herself studying the pattern on the carpet, because she couldn't bring herself to look into his eyes.

He emitted a light chuckle. "There's nothing to apologize for. I enjoyed it, and I'm pretty sure you did, too."

"That's not the point."

Another deep chuckle. "So you admit that you enjoyed it."

She sighed. *It's too early in the morning for this.* "Mr. Alvarez, please. I just wanted to make sure we're on the same page, and that we're not going to let it happen again."

A few moments passed in silence and she entertained herself by counting floor tiles. She couldn't remember ever feeling this conflicted before.

"Look at me, Joi. I want to talk to you, not the top of your head."

She slowly looked up, and as their eyes met she in-

stantly regretted it. In his eyes, she saw the same un-
masked attraction she'd seen the previous day, in the
moment before their lips met.

"It's obvious there's something between us, but you
seem bent on denying it. Why can't we just enjoy each
other, with no strings and no commitments?"

She blinked twice. "I don't do that, Mr. Alvarez.
I'm not into random hookups. And as I said, I'm not
interested in clouding your judgment when the time
comes to decide whether Citadel earns this contract
on a permanent basis."

He drew in a deep breath, accompanied by a slow
bob of his head. "Very well. I'll respect your wishes
to keep things professional."

"I would really appreciate that."

"I don't want to make you uncomfortable, so I won't
make any teasing remarks, or kiss you again, unless
you ask me to."

She blew out a breath, filled with a modicum of relief. "Thank you."

"All I ask is that you call me Marco. This 'Mr. Alvarez' stuff is more appropriate for my father. Deal?"

"Deal."

She was glad they'd come to an agreement, and she
was determined to hold up her end. If he really planned
to wait until she asked him to kiss her, then the problem was solved. At least that's what the logical parts
of her wanted to believe.

She turned and headed out of the office, knowing
that if she stayed, she only ran the risk of saying or
doing something she had no business saying or doing.

"I'm better at keeping my word than you are, by
the way."

There was an accusatory edge to his tone that she didn't appreciate. It raised her hackles, and she wanted to turn around and tell him about himself. But the day had to start at some point, and she'd already been in the room with him long enough.

With her back still turned to him, she said, "We'll see."

Without so much as a glance in his direction, she made her way down the corridor.

After Joi stalked out of his office, Marco shook his head. She was determined to deny what was going on between them, no matter how impossible that task might be.

When he thought about it, she was probably doing the right thing. After all, he knew very little about her, and what he did know was old information. Six years ago, he'd watched her walk down the aisle to marry his college roommate. Less than fifteen minutes later, he'd watched her turn and sprint back down that very same aisle, leaving behind her bouquet, one hundred confused guests and a shocked and embarrassed would-be groom. From that incident, he'd drawn two conclusions about her. One, she didn't do well with commitment, and two, she excelled at keeping secrets and playing a role.

Considering those events, he wondered why he was even attracted to her. His mind knew better than to trust her, but his body had betrayed him by giving in to the inexplicable fascination he had with her. He stood from his spot on the edge of his desk, taking a few steps toward his bookcase. On the wall next to the five-shelf unit hung his degrees; his bachelor's degree in economic sciences from the University of Costa Rica at San Pedro, and his MBA from the Stern School of Business at New York University. He thought back on his college days, a welcome distraction from pondering over the dilemma presented by his new security contractor. Those days had been filled with all-nighters in the library, and while he'd been a good student, he'd rarely been alone during those late-night study sessions. Women had seemed to fall into his arms on command back then, a trend that had continued into the present. Before Joi came along, no woman had ever turned him down quite so flatly.

Pushing those thoughts away, he reached to the second shelf and took down the volume he wanted. With the binder containing the quarterly reports from the previous year in hand, he went back to his desk and pulled his chair out.

Before he could sit, though, Roosevelt swung his office door open and came inside. "Marco, we've got a situation out here."

Sensing the urgency in Roosevelt's tone, Marco stood up straight. "What's going on?"

"We've got a couple of guys harassing an elderly lady in the parking lot."

Before Roosevelt could finish his sentence, Marco had already moved around his desk. They both jogged down the corridor, past the vault and the offices and through the lobby. As they moved, Marco looked around for Joi, or one of the guards, but saw no sign of any of them. He felt his brow crease with irritation. *Where the hell is my security staff?*

Marco reached the main entrance first, and swung open the door. As he and Roosevelt rushed out onto the sidewalk, he scanned the parking lot for the trouble-makers, and for his customer, to make sure she was safe.

Roosevelt swung his arm out to cease Marco's for-ward momentum. "Marco. Look."

Marco swiveled his head to the left, in the direction Roosevelt indicated.

He turned just in time to see Joi perform a takedown move on a tall, well-built man. The man went down like a fallen tower, and Joi was on him right away, ensuring that he wouldn't get up again until she was good and ready.

Behind her, he could see Yolanda kneeling on the ground. She had a second young man pinned to the sidewalk.

As for the elderly customer, she was standing nearby, watching. A look of righteous satisfaction spread over her aged face.

Marco moved closer, to get a better view of the situ-ation. When he came abreast of the fracas, he could see that both Yolanda and Joi were employing some sort of submission hold on the two hapless perpetrators, each of whom were lying on their backs on the concrete.

"Yolanda, zip ties, please." Joi reached out to her employee.

"Got 'em right here." Yolanda used one hand to reach into one of the pockets of her utility belt and produced two bright yellow plastic ties, one of which she handed to Joi.

Marco watched as the two fair-haired, red-faced men were sat up by the women, who then secured their wrists behind their backs.

Yolanda, back on her feet now, already had her

phone out. "I'll get the police over here to round them up." She reached out a hand, and helped her boss to her feet.

"Thanks." Joi took the offered help, then dusted the grains of dirt from the knees of her uniform slacks.

Marco blinked a few times, taking it all in. He'd just watched Joi put a hold on a man who was easily twice her size, and as far as he could tell, she hadn't even mussed her hair in the process. There was nothing he could do but stare in wonder. Everything she'd said during her proposal about not being afraid of physical confrontation had just been proven true, right before his eyes.

Roosevelt, with a wide grin on his face, gave Joi a fist bump. "Nice work, Ms. Lewis."

She returned the gesture with a smile of her own. "No biggie. Just a typical Wednesday at work, right, Yolanda?"

The guard winked. "Sure is, boss lady."

At that moment, Jackie, the other guard, stuck her head out the door. "Oh, I missed it. Y'all got it under control out there?"

"We're good, Jackie," Joi called. "Just waiting for the fuzz."

"Gotcha." And she disappeared back inside.

Marco shook his head in amazement. "Ms. Lewis, I'm very impressed."

In response, Joi chuckled. "You should see me when I've had espresso."

The arrival of a black-and-white Charlotte Police cruiser interrupted their exchange. Marco stayed close by while the two men in zip ties were loaded into the car, in case the police needed anything from him.

One of the two police officers asked, "Mr. Alvarez, would you like to file a report?"

"Yes, I would." Marco reached into the inner pocket of his blazer for a pen.

Joi stepped between them. "Officer, I'm Joi Lewis of Citadel Security. Royal Bank is under our protection, so my staff will complete any necessary paperwork on behalf of our client."

An outdone Marco tucked the pen back into his pocket. *She's really on top of things.* In light of that, he took a step back and allowed her the space she needed to do her job. Her capabilities were on full display, and he was content to observe her without interfering. All the while, he noted how confident and poised she appeared, despite having wrestled a pretty sizable man to the ground only a few minutes ago.

The officer extended the clipboard tucked beneath his arm to Joi. "Okay, ma'am. Here's everything I need to have completed to make my report."

"No problem. My staff and I will have these forms completed and delivered to your office at the police station within two hours. Will that be sufficient?"

"Yes, ma'am. Thank you."

"No problem, sir." Joi took the clipboard, and snatched a pen from behind her ear. "Let me take down your information."

After a brief conversation with Joi, the officer returned to his cruiser. A few minutes later, the cruiser backed out of the space and pulled out of the parking lot.

Marco turned again, thinking he'd make sure the customer was all right, but he saw Roosevelt already walking the woman to her car. From what he could tell, there was nothing for him to do but return to his office, and the endless stack of paperwork waiting for him there.

When he approached the main entrance door, Joi was already there.

Holding it open as he reentered the bank, she remarked, "I may need your signature on these forms. I'll bring them to your office once everything else is filled out."

As the door swung shut behind them, he leaned near her ear. "That was some hell of a takedown."

A soft smile graced her face. "You'll do well to remember that, so I won't have to use it on you."

He grimaced and took a big step away from her. "You'd injure me, fair damsel?"

"Like I said, I'll bring you the paperwork when it's done." Shaking her head, she strolled away.

He watched the sway of her retreating hips with appreciative eyes, and wondered what other hidden skills she possessed.

Chapter 7

Cup of coffee in hand, Joi took a seat in the lobby of the Citadel Security office. She'd pulled up the Thursday morning episode of *News One Now* on her tablet, and watched it as she waited for her interviewee to arrive. The appointment was set for eight thirty, so she expected to have at least twenty more minutes of solitude before Karen came in.

As her routine dictated whenever her guards took on a new contract, she planned to spend a couple of hours at the office before heading to the bank. She'd spend the rest of the day with her staff at the worksite, and continue to do that through the trial period. It was her way of making sure things ran smoothly, because despite her confidence in her guards, she was always extra cautious when they began a new job.

When the episode of the news show ended, Joi shut

down her tablet and looked up. *No sign of Karen. I wonder what's going on.* In the eight years they'd been in business together, Karen had only been late to work twice. Both times, she'd been involved in a mishap of some kind. Punctuality was Karen's hallmark, so any time she was late, Joi got worried. Reaching into her purse, she fished out her smartphone, preparing to search for Karen's contact.

Before she could unlock the screen, an incoming call flashed on the display. Swiping, she answered it. "Hello?"

"Hey, Joi. It's Gabe."

Hearing the voice of Karen's husband on the other end of the line made Joi's hair stand on end. "Oh, God, Gabe. What's happened to Karen?"

"Nothing too serious, but she did take a fall this morning. We're at an urgent care now, but we're being transferred to the hospital."

"A fall? Where?"

"At the house. She slipped on a patch of ice in the driveway."

That didn't surprise her, considering last night's weather. It had been unseasonably cold, with temperatures dropping down into the teens. "How bad is it?"

"I'm not really sure, but she's probably broken her arm. They've got it in a sling right now."

She sucked in a breath, glad that some of the neighborhood kids had come by to salt her driveway and sidewalk yesterday afternoon. "Ouch. What hospital is she going to?"

"Carolinas, in Pineville." Gabe's voice conveyed the concern he had for his wife. "I've already taken the

day off from the optical shop so I can stay with her."
Gabe was an ophthalmologist by trade.

"Good. Look, I've got an interviewee coming in
any minute, but as soon as I'm finished with that, I'll
be over to check on Karen."

"I'll let her know."

"Give her my love, Gabe."

"I will." He disconnected the call.

Joi sighed aloud, releasing the sound into the empty
lobby. She hoped Karen wasn't in too much pain, because it sounded like she'd taken quite a spill. Now
she'd have to calm her nerves, because she still needed
to be able to focus on the interview she was about to
conduct.

Since this turn of events meant she wouldn't make
it to Royal until much later than she'd intended, she
put in a call to the bank. After informing Roosevelt
of the situation, and asking him to pass her message
on to Marco, she tucked her phone back into her purse
and went to refill her coffee mug.

By the time she returned from the break room, she
heard the bell chime over the door. She crossed the
lobby, her free hand extended toward her interviewee.
"Ms. Mendez?"

"Yes." The woman, who was of average height and
slender build, had fiery red hair and a bright smile. She
reached out to give Joi a firm handshake. "You must
be Ms. Lewis. Good morning."

"Good morning. Come on in and have a seat."

The two of them sat across from each other in up-
holstered chairs in the lobby, with a short-legged coffee table between them.

Joi asked, "Would you like a cup of coffee, Ms. Mendez? There's a fresh pot in the break room."

"No, thanks. I'm more of a tea drinker, but I'm good for now." She settled back into the cushion of her chair. "And please, call me Maravillosa."

"That's a beautiful name, by the way. It means 'wonderful,' doesn't it?"

Maravillosa responded with an easy grin. "Yes, it does, and thank you."

Taking the resume out of a folder she'd laid on the table earlier, Joi began the interview by going over some of Maravillosa's experience. "I see you're an Air Force veteran. I've never had the pleasure of having one on my staff."

"Yes, ma'am. I served fifteen years as a 3POX1B combat training and maintenance specialist."

They spent the next half an hour talking about Maravillosa's time in the service, her career goals and why she'd applied for the position. Joi did her best to be attentive as Maravillosa answered her questions, but part of her mind was distracted by her worries about Karen.

Finally, Joi stood. "Maravillosa, I think you might be a good fit for Citadel, but I'll need to discuss this with my partner. We'll be in touch with you soon."

Maravillosa gave her another firm handshake. "Thanks so much for your time, ma'am. I look forward to hearing from you."

With a wave, Maravillosa Mendez pushed open the door and left the office. Joi returned to the break room, fetching her pea coat from the coatrack. Once she'd slipped into it, she placed a wool beret atop her hair, pulled on a pair of red leather gloves and grabbed her purse from the chair she'd been sitting in. Pushing the door open, she frowned at the cold blast of air that met her, then hurried to her truck.

Morning rush hour in downtown Charlotte had come to an end, so it took her less than fifteen minutes to reach the hospital. After she parked, she entered the building and went straight to the nearest information desk to find out where Karen was. The man there directed her to the orthopedic unit on the third floor. Finding out Karen's location from the serious-looking nurse at the station took longer than it had to navigate the city streets. After butting up against the nurse's insistent declarations about hospital privacy laws for a full fifteen minutes, Joi put in a call to Gabe and asked him to pull some strings. The phone rang behind the nurse's station, and the salty lady in scrubs took the call. After a brief conversation with the person on the other line, the nurse finally directed Joi to Karen's room.

Entering the room a few minutes later, Joi was relieved to see Karen sitting up in bed. Her dutiful husband kept watch over her from his seat in an armless chair to the right of her bed. Karen's right arm was indeed in a sling, but other than that, she seemed to be okay.

Standing by the left side of the bed, Joi grasped Karen's free hand. "Girl, you scared me. How are you feeling?"

Karen grimaced. "I've been better, but the pain meds they gave me are starting to kick in. Finally."

"Gabe says you slipped. How bad was it?"

"I was outside rinsing mud off my undercarriage yesterday. I wasn't really thinking about how cold it would get last night." Karen shifted in bed, and grimaced again.

Gabe was at her side in a flash. "Baby, you've got to stop squirming. I don't want you to make the injury any worse."

Karen rolled her eyes, but leaned in slightly to accept her husband's kiss on the cheek. "See what I have to put up with? I'm incapacitated and he's still policing me."

Joi shook her head, chuckling at their interaction. "Has a doctor seen her here yet? What do we know about what's wrong?"

Gabe replied, "They've taken an X-ray, and we're waiting for the results. But like I said, something's probably broken. You don't want to see what her arm looks like underneath that sling." He frowned.

"Ouch." Joi tsked, shaking her head.

"I am in the room, you know. You could just ask me." Karen stuck her lips out in a mock pout.

"Hush, before I go after the other arm," Joi chided.

Joi hung around for about an hour, during which she got to hear the doctor's report. Karen's right wrist was indeed broken, and she'd also dislocated her shoulder. All told, she would need to be out of work for at least two weeks, maybe longer.

After the doctor left, Karen turned to Joi with a guilty look on her face. "Geez, Joi, I'm sorry about this. We've just taken on a new contract, and now I'm going to be out of commission."

Joi waved her off. "Don't worry about it. I've still got your assistant to help me with the tech stuff, and I'm fully staffed on guards. I'll be fine until you get back."

Karen didn't look particularly convinced. "Are you sure? Because maybe I can telecommute, and use one of those dictation programs to…"

"No. I want you to concentrate on getting better. If I need you, I'll call you, but only if it's absolutely necessary."

"But, Joi, I…"

Joi silenced her friend and business partner with a cutting look. "Rest, Karen." She turned to Gabe. "Will you do me a favor and make sure your wife gets her rest?"

Gabe nodded. "You know I will."

"Good. I'll swing by the house in a few days to check in with you, okay?"

Knowing she'd lost the battle, Karen sighed. "Okay. I'll be good."

Satisfied, Joi gave Karen's hand a squeeze. "Then I'll see you later. I've got to get over to the bank."

With a wave to Karen and Gabe, Joi slipped out of the room.

With the wooden reed to his saxophone sticking out of his mouth, Marco settled onto the stool in front of his music stand. He wore his neck strap loosely around his collarbone, securing his control of the sax. He and the Gents were set up in the music room in his house for their weekly Saturday rehearsal. The spare bedroom, with its large bay window and high ceiling, provided the perfect acoustics and lighting for the band to practice.

Once he deemed the reed properly dampened, he set in the mouthpiece of his sax and tightened the gold screws that held it in place. Putting the mouthpiece between his lips, he blew into it, playing a middle C. Not liking the way it sounded, he continued to blow, stopping periodically to make adjustments.

Across from him, Darius was ensconced in the window seat, setting up Miss Molly, his beloved upright bass. Ken had already set up his drums, and busied himself tapping out a rhythm on the snare and high hat cymbal. Rashad sat on the bench in front of Marco's aged upright piano, picking out a few notes to test the tune of the old eighty-eights.

Darius's voice broke the near silence in the room. "Are we going to do the Cole Porter set this week? We had a lot of requests for it last week."

Marco shrugged. "It's fine by me, if that's what the ladies want."

Ken chuckled. "Heaven forbid you don't deliver what the ladies want."

A few snickers broke out in the room, and Marco cut his eyes at the drummer. "Shut up, Ken."

Rashad, still tapping keys on the piano, spoke then. "I'm going to guess you're not having an easy time with your new security contractor."

Marco rolled his eyes. He'd hoped to avoid that particular subject today. "I don't want to talk about it."

"Oh, come on, Marco. You're the one who's always bragging about being a ladies' man. Now you want to clam up, the one time we're actually interested?" Darius gave him a look of amusement from his perch in the window seat.

Rather than answer, Marco attempted a middle C from the saxophone but it still didn't sound quite right to him.

"Darius is right," Rashad remarked. "Does this mean Ms. Lewis is immune to your many charms?"

Marco let the mouthpiece fall from his mouth, and rested his sax against his right hip. "No, she's a woman just like the rest of them." That statement was only partially true. Yes, Joi Lewis was a woman, but there was something about her, some appealing quality that set her apart from her peers.

"Really, Marco?" Darius folded his arms over his chest, looking very much unconvinced.

"She's not immune. She's just…stubborn." It was the truth. Marco had never encountered a woman so determined to dismiss his many positive qualities.

Another round of chuckles filled the room.

"It's true," Marco groused. "She's already admitted she's attracted to me, but she's decided to ignore it."

"Why?" Darius's tone was mocking.

"She wants to keep things strictly professional between us, because she doesn't want any preferential treatment when her company's trial period is up."

"I don't see why you're complaining. She's doing the right thing, and possibly saving the both of you from a potentially awkward situation." That comment came from Ken, who'd laid down his drumsticks and was now shuffling through pages of sheet music.

"It's too late for that." Marco wanted to elaborate, and tell Ken that things between him and Joi were already plenty awkward. But he knew there was no point. His friends, in typical Gents fashion, were going to keep entertaining themselves at his expense, at least until someone changed the subject.

"Did you get a chance to kiss her? That usually

turns women into putty in your hands, right?" The snide question came from Rashad.

He recalled the kiss they'd shared. The memory of the softness of her lips was particularly potent. "Yes, I kissed her. And you can now stop being an ass about this, before I use your locks to strangle you." Marco cut a censuring look in Rashad's direction.

Darius cut in. "All right, guys. I think we've teased Marco enough. We need to start deciding on a set list and a stage costume for the Winter Jazz Fest, and then we need to actually practice so we don't sound terrible when we take the stage this week."

Marco listened as his bandmates went back and forth about the upcoming jazz festival, relieved that the heat was finally off him. The four of them conversed for several minutes about what songs they would play, and how they would alter their usual stage wear for the event. The Winter Jazz Fest typically drew large crowds numbering in the thousands. Getting in front of an audience that large was a big deal for the Gents. While none of them considered themselves career musicians, they all agreed that their love of the music made them want to reach as many people as they could.

"All right, so we'll do a few original songs, and round the set out with the crowd-pleasers—Monk, Miles and Coltrane." Darius jotted the tentative set list on a legal pad. "Sound good?"

Everyone agreed.

"Great, now let's practice. We'll run through 'Anything Goes' first. Count us off, Ken."

As the men readied their instruments, Ken raised his sticks above his head, crossing them in a V formation. Tapping them together, he gave the count. "Five, four, three, two."

All of them began to play their respective parts, the sound blending together to provide a pleasing back-drop to Rashad's impassioned crooning.

The sound was, quite literally, music to Marco's ears. As he moved his fingers over the keys of his saxophone, turning his breath into the clear notes sup-porting the harmony, he felt a certain joy rising inside. This level of peace was something he only achieved when he played his sax, and if it were possible, he'd live there. And when the notes from his sax joined with Rashad's skillful piano playing, the deep notes echoing from Darius's fingers playing over the strings of his bass and the rhythmic cadence of Ken's drums, they created something truly magical. Each man played off the other, combining their talents to give new life to the classic jazz compositions they all knew and loved.

When the first song ended, a collective cheer went up in the room.

Rashad had a broad grin on his face. "Damn. We're hot today, y'all."

Marco had to agree. He imagined his own play-ing might have been affected by the song's lyrics and meaning, and how it related to his current feelings about Joi. But since he'd survived his friends' earlier barrage of questions, he knew better than to bring the subject back up again.

The band moved on to the next song, Cole Porter's classic, "Night and Day." As Marco played the notes, he continued to let his passion for the music, and his growing fascination with Joi, inform his execution. She might never come around, but at least he'd have the inspiration she provided to fuel him toward the pinnacle of his talents.

Knowing that made him feel somewhat better, so he smiled around the mouthpiece of the sax, and gave it his all.

Chapter 8

Monday morning, Joi arrived at the bank twenty minutes before opening time. She, Jackie and Yolanda made small talk as they sat on the bench outside, waiting for Marco and Roosevelt to show up with the keys. Joi smiled through the entire conversation, because she genuinely enjoyed the company of her guards, and considered them friends as well as employees. Beneath her smile, though, were the hidden feelings she harbored for the bank's president. But she would never share those feelings with her guards—things were awkward enough for her at the bank as it was. She'd only confided in Joanne because she knew she could trust her older sister, both to keep her secret and to give her sound advice.

When the two men approached the door, the women ceased their chatting. One by one, they stood, awaiting entrance to the bank.

Joi stood last, brushing a hand over her long hounds-tooth coat to release the wrinkles from it. *Am I primping for him?* As soon as the question entered her mind, she pushed it away. She was merely maintaining a professional appearance. Her efforts had everything to do with being a businesswoman, and nothing to do with the dark-haired banker.

"Good morning, ladies." The deep, silken tone of Marco's voice cut through the chill of the early-morning air, warming Joi's insides.

Everyone exchanged pleasantries, but Joi's eyes were on Marco.

When their gazes locked, time seemed to stand still. There was something in his eyes, something that called to her.

Still staring into her eyes, he swung open the door, and held it open. "Ladies first."

Yolanda and Jackie went in right away, but Joi lingered. Enraptured by his gaze, she felt as if her feet were rooted to the spot she occupied on the concrete sidewalk. She could feel the warmth of the bank's heated interior flowing out through the door. But that electrically generated heat was no match for the heat she felt blooming inside, as she gazed into Marco's eyes.

Marco stared back. His gaze was intense, and seemed to hold the weight of words that were going unsaid.

Suddenly she heard the sound of someone clearing their throat.

A few long beats passed before she realized Roosevelt was still standing there with them. Roosevelt's crooked smile conveyed a sense of mirth, and of knowing.

Shaking her head, she blinked a few times to break

the spell. "Excuse me, gentlemen." Careful to avoid any contact between her body and Marco's, she eased past him and slipped inside the building.

She heard Marco chuckle as she retreated, making a beeline for the ladies' room. As insistent as Marco could be, she knew he wouldn't follow her in there.

Within the confines of the restroom, she stood by the mirror and looked at her reflection. Her eyes were watering a bit, so she dried them with a paper towel from the dispenser, careful not to disturb the thin layer of pressed powder she wore to keep somewhat oily skin at bay. After retouching her lip gloss, she took a few deep, cleansing breaths, then walked out.

And cursed under her breath when she saw Marco standing outside the loan officer's door, directly across from the ladies' room.

Was he waiting for me? She knew it was possible that he had some business to discuss with the loan officer, or some other reason he should be standing in that very spot. But that didn't keep her from being a bit suspicious of his motives.

Her suspicion only increased when he caught sight of her and immediately began walking in her direction.

A part of her wanted to flee, but she stayed where she was. She'd already run from him once today, and she didn't want to make a habit of that. Beyond that, he'd made it obvious that he wouldn't be deterred, at least not while they were both in the building.

So she watched him striding in her direction, awaiting whatever he might have to say. She couldn't help but notice the way the tailored dark navy suit fit his athletic frame. The fabric at the forearms stretched ever so slightly to accommodate his biceps. From the crown of his dark waves of luscious black hair, to the smart blue paisley tie and the designer leather dress shoes on his feet, he was about as handsome and impeccably dressed as a man could be.

As he entered her space, her eyes focused on the masculine lines of his face. His square jaw was bare, shaved of any facial hair. Generally, she liked for a man to have a bit of scruff, but on Marco, she found the clean-shaven look surprisingly appealing.

His cocoa-dark eyes held evidence of his humor as he spoke. "Ms. Lewis. If I didn't know better, I might think you were avoiding me."

She gave him a half smirk, but said nothing.

"Come on, Joi. I thought you were made of tougher stuff."

Folding her arms over her chest, she quipped, "I am, and you'd better remember that."

He smiled, while scratching his chin. "Oh, don't worry. You don't have to remind me about your black belt. Not after the way you took that guy down last week." He scrunched his face into a pained expression.

A peal of laughter escaped her throat, in response to the face he made. "Honestly, Marco…"

"Aha! So you *can* call me by my first name."

"That was our deal, wasn't it? I'd call you Marco if you agreed not to pursue me."

He held up his index finger, wiggling it from side to side. "I agreed not to pursue you, *unless you asked.*"

She shrugged. "Same difference."

He took a small step forward, coming within a few inches of where she stood.

The heat of his body seemed to reach out, whispering over her like a lover's caress. A sensual shiver ran through her, radiating from her core out to the tips of her fingers and toes. Despite his casual demeanor, he seemed to be wielding a strange, erotic power over her. The space between them notwithstanding, she felt as if he were touching her. Or was that just her mind, carrying her off to fantasy land again?

"I'm a man of my word, Joi. You can be assured I will not do or say anything to you unless I'm asked." His words held credence and weight.

She could sense his honesty, and she responded with a slow nod. "Thank you, Marco."

With a nod of his own, he backed up, taking his incredible body heat with him. "Have a good day, Joi."

She watched him walk away, this time feasting her eyes on the rear view of him in the snazzy suit. She could see the outline of his powerful thighs, and a rear end so nice, she had to look twice.

She closed her eyes briefly, knowing she needed to stop ogling him and get her focus back on the work ahead.

Joi, you will not spend the entire day thinking about this man.

That was what she told herself, but she could already tell that today would indeed be a manic Monday.

Within the quiet confines of his office, Marco worked on his computer. He'd taken off his sport coat and tossed it over the back of his chair, in anticipation of an intense work session. His tie loosened and his shoes on the floor beside the desk, he'd proceeded to dive headfirst into his duties. By lunchtime, he realized he'd be stuck at his desk for at least another hour if he wanted to get the task done.

He ordered in for lunch, and after he'd finished his meal of a grilled chicken sandwich and a cup of French onion soup, he moved on to the rest of the day's work.

Around two, he'd completed the current stack and cleared the clutter from his desk, but it was a hollow victory. He knew that in two or three days, the stack would be replaced by another one just as tall.

He stifled a yawn, then got up from his desk to stretch. Just as he raised his arms over his head, his smartphone rang.

He reached into the hip pocket of his trousers and took out the phone. Looking at the name and number, he felt his brow rise in shock. With a swipe of his finger, he answered the call. "Ernesto? How the hell are you, man?"

On the other end of the line, his friend laughed. "I'm doing great, Marco. How are you, you SOB?"

Now it was Marco's turn to laugh. "I'm fine. It's been a long time, E. What brings you out of the woodwork?"

"I know, man. I wanted to invite you to my parents' party. They're celebrating forty years in the pineapple business."

His brow hitched again when he heard that. Ernesto's parents, Enrique and Consuela Herrera, owned the largest pineapple empire in Costa Rica. The Herreras had their hand in everything, from growing the fruit, to harvesting, processing and packing. With pineapples being Costa Rica's second-largest export crop, behind bananas, the Herrera family enjoyed incredible wealth and status in their home country. "Is this party being held back home in Limón?"

"You bet your ass. Where else would they have it? They've booked the Tortuga Lodge ballroom."

"When is it?" As homesick as he was, Marco would take any excuse to escape the frigid North Carolina winds and visit his coastal home.

"A week from now. Can you make it?"

"That's pretty short notice, Ernesto." He'd already decided he would attend the party, but he enjoyed making his friend sweat it out.

"Aw, come on. Mama is always going on about you. She knows that if it wasn't for you keeping me focused back in college, I would never have graduated." Ernesto's voice held an edge of guilt.

"She's right. You were a total slacker. But what are friends for?"

Ernesto sighed. "All right, all right. I'm forever in your debt. Now will you come to the party?"

He laughed, standing by the window in his office. His hand brushed against the glass, and feeling the cold clinging to the windowpane sealed the deal for him. "Sure, Ernesto. I'll have to make some arrangements around here, but tell Mama Herrera I'll be there."

"Great. Thanks, man. Should I tell her to give you a plus-one?"

He ran his free hand through his hair. There was only one person he would want to escort to the Herreras' party, and he was pretty sure she'd slap him if he asked. Still, he wasn't about to admit that to his friend, so he said, "Of course. When have you ever known me to attend an event alone?"

A snickering Ernesto responded, "Never. Remember that homecoming dance in college, when you took two dates?"

The memory of that night was still fresh, and it brought a smile to Marco's face. That night, more than a decade ago, he'd entered the university gymnasium with a woman on each of his arms. He couldn't remember their names. "Yes, I recall. One was fair and blonde. The other was tan with dark hair."

"You're getting old, man."

"Speak for yourself. I'm at the office, Ernesto, so I'll talk to you later."

"Gotcha. Later, Marco."

When Marco ended the call and pocketed his phone again, he found himself chuckling. It seemed his college buddy was just as much of a procrastinator as he'd always been. Who else would give a person less than two weeks' notice to make an international trip? He made a note to box Ernesto's ears when he saw him next.

Thinking of Ernesto and their past together inevitably brought Joi to mind. Back then, she'd been Ernesto's reserved yet lovely fiancée. Ernesto had been ready to commit to her, for reasons Marco was well aware of. That is, up until the day she'd bolted from the altar, leaving behind any possibility of the future they might have had together.

He wondered if she ever regretted her decision, or if she ever questioned why Ernesto never made a real effort to contact her after she abandoned him.

He knew. He knew it all, and he suspected she was none the wiser. No, she couldn't have known Ernesto's motivation for getting married. No one, other than Marco and Ernesto himself, knew that Ernesto needed a wife so that he could claim his inheritance to the Herrera pineapple fortune.

Still, Marco had heard of woman's intuition. Had she run because she'd sensed that Ernesto's love wasn't real? Did she somehow know that while he had proposed, and pledged his fidelity, that he would never truly be committed to her?

On Ernesto and Joi's wedding day, she'd only made it halfway down the aisle before she stopped, turned and sprinted out of the church. Standing next to his friend, Marco had watched her go, then tried to comfort Ernesto. All the while, he knew that if Ernesto hadn't approached Joi first, he would have gone after her. Why had fate chosen to drop her back in his life again?

There was no way for him to know the answers to those questions, and he certainly wouldn't ask her. Doing so would mean admitting to her that he'd played a role in Ernesto's plan of deception. After the way he'd treated her, announcing his mistrust at every opportunity, he knew she'd think of him as nothing more than a hypocritical liar. And in a way, she'd be right.

A knock on his office door drew him out of his thoughts and back to reality. Turning from the window to face the door, he said, "Come in."

Nancy, one of the tellers, stuck her head in the door. "Mr. Alvarez, we've got a new customer out front who wants to meet you."

"I'll be there in a second, Nancy."

She stepped back and closed the door.

Marco stepped into his shoes, retightened his tie and pulled on his sport jacket. He glanced at his reflection in the wall mirror hanging by his bookshelf, and once he'd smoothed the lines out of his suit, he left his office for the lobby.

Nancy, who'd returned to her station, gestured to a young girl standing by the teller desk.

Marco strolled over to the girl, who was no more than ten. She wore her hair in two curly Afro puffs. She had a ceramic piggy bank tucked under one arm, and a very serious look on her young face.

Joi stood next to the girl, with a sweet smile on her beautiful face that seemed to be directed at the youngster.

Marco extended his hand to the girl, wearing a smile of his own. "Hello, ma'am. I'm Mr. Alvarez. My teller said you wanted to meet me."

She stuck out her hand and shook his. "Are you the bank boss?"

"Yes, I'm president of the bank. How can I help you?"

The young girl showed him her piggy bank. "This is all my lemonade stand money, for three summers. If I'm gonna deposit it here, my daddy says I need to know the man who runs the place, and shake his hand."

"Sounds like your dad's a smart man. I'd be honored to have you as a customer, Miss…"

She grinned. "Oh, sorry. My name is Tia Jackson."

"Well, welcome, Ms. Jackson." Marco stood, gesturing to Joi. "This is our security chief, Ms. Lewis. She'll be in charge of making sure your money is kept safe."

Joi cut him a sidelong glance, but turned to Tia with a pleasant expression. "That's right. And I have a staff to help me do it, so we'll make sure your money stays in the vault until you're ready to take it out."

Tia looked between the two of them. Seemingly satisfied, she moved up to Nancy's teller station. "Ms.

Nancy, I'd like to make my deposit now." Carefully, she placed the piggy bank on the desk.

Out of the corner of his eye, Marco could see a dark-skinned man of average height, watching the exchange from a short distance away. The man's features were so reminiscent of young Tia's, Marco knew the man must be her father. He walked over and had a brief chat with Mr. Jackson, complimenting him on his daughter's savvy. A few minutes later, he watched the two of them leave, with Tia proudly clutching her empty piggy bank and her very first deposit slip.

That evening, as he locked up the bank's doors, he turned to see Joi, tucking her things into the passenger seat of her pickup truck. The early evening had given way to darkness, but the lamps in the parking lot cast pools of bluish light all over the area.

She closed the door, and spotted him.

Tucking away the bank keys, he gave her a wave.

He thought she'd wave back and climb into her truck. Instead, she meandered over to where he stood on the sidewalk.

"You were pretty good with Ms. Jackson," she remarked, in reference to the young depositor.

"Thanks, but I treat all my customers with equal respect." He looked down into her eyes, searching for the real reason she'd come over to him. He sensed this small talk wasn't it.

She looked down, and he could see the dark fringe of her lashes fluttering. "I'm having a hard time with this."

"With what?"

"With not asking you to kiss me again."

His blood warmed. "Then ask me, and I'll cure you."

She raised her gaze to his again, with desire sparkling in her eyes. Her gloved hands came to rest on his forearms as she whispered, "Kiss me, Marco."

So he did. He dipped his head, letting his lips crush against hers. The kiss was potent, and filled with unspoken wanting.

When they parted, he saw her safely to her truck.

Then, with the moon hanging high in the winter night sky, he watched her drive away.

Chapter 9

Every other Wednesday, Joi had a standing movie date with her sister, Joanne. The two of them would get together at Joi's house, away from Joanne's husband and son, and enjoy whatever mushy chick flick they chose. They'd begun the tradition a couple of years ago, and had used Joanne's house until the male complaints there began to take some of the fun out of their movie viewing.

This week's selection was *Mahogany*, a classic that Joi could never tire of. She was lounging in her recliner in the living room of her ranch-style house, wrapped in a plaid fleece throw. A bowl of popcorn sat in her lap, and a mug of hot tea was perched on the folding table nearby.

Joanne lay stretched out on the sofa, with a pillow propped behind her back. She sipped from a chilled glass of rosé, and munched on a bowl of snack mix as they watched the movie on Joi's forty-six-inch flat-screen television.

Even though the movie was one of her favorites, Joi's focus was tenuous at best. She couldn't shake the memory of the kiss she'd shared with Marco two nights prior. He'd been gentle, yet passionate, his lips awakening a level of desire in her she hadn't known she could reach.

On screen, the two main characters were locked in a passionate embrace. Joi couldn't stop her mind from drifting, imagining what it would be like to be with Marco that way. Would he be as gentle and passionate a lover as his kiss had alluded to?

A throw pillow came out of nowhere, flying across the room, and hit Joi in the head.

She jerked her head toward Joanne, who was now sitting up and looking directly at her.

Joi tossed the pillow back at her sister. "What was that for? Do you know how uncouth it is to attack me in my own house, with my own pillow?"

Joanne caught the pillow, and replaced it on the sofa. "I don't know, but I guess it's about as rude as inviting me over here to watch a movie, and then daydreaming the whole time."

Joi dropped her eyes. "Not the whole time."

"Whatever. If you expect me to sit through this movie for the umpteenth time, the least you could do is watch it."

"*Mahogany* is a classic, Joanne."

She scoffed. "Maybe for the first five or ten viewings. After that, it loses its luster, Joi."

"Sorry." Joi knew her older sister would expect her to apologize, and she hoped that would be enough.

It wasn't.

With her arms folded over her chest, Joanne fixed her with a serious glare. "Joi, what is going on with you?"

Eyes darting from left to right, in search of a quick escape route, Joi tried to keep her tone casual. "Um, nothing. Everything's fine."

Joanne pursed her lips tighter than a too-small pair of jeans. "Girl, you are lying!"

She shrank back and drew the throw closer around her body. "I am not."

"Yes, you are. I can tell, because your eye is twitching. You're doing the shifty-eye lie twitch!"

"No, I'm not." She knew she was telling a lie before the words formed. At times like this, she hated how well her sister knew her. Just once, she'd like to know what it felt like to keep a secret from Joanne, though deep down she knew she told her sister just about everything.

Joanne said nothing, but wagged her index finger in Joi's direction, still frowning.

Joi rolled her eyes. "Damn, Jo, you're worse than Mom. Will you put that finger away?"

"Tell me the truth and I will."

Sinking down into the soft cushion of her recliner, Joi sighed. "Fine. I kissed Marco. Again. Are you happy now?"

Joanne retracted her accusatory finger, as promised. Grabbing the remote, she paused the movie. "No, I'm not happy. I thought we had this conversation already?"

"We did," Joi murmured.

"And I thought we both agreed that you should keep things strictly professional between you and Marco."

"We did."

"Well, what the hell happened?" Joanne leaned back against the sofa cushions with an expectant expression.

"Well…"

"Don't clam up on me now. Tell me what's going on between the two of you."

"You saw him. He's so handsome it hurts my eyes."

Joanne groaned. "I'm not disputing that. The man is fine. But if you screw up and lose this contract, it's going to hurt your pockets. Not to mention your guard staff, and poor Karen."

Joi didn't have a ready comeback for that. She should have seen it coming, because her sister was a master at laying on the guilt.

"You don't want your whole staff to be out of work, Joi. And when Karen does get better, I'm guessing she'd like to still have a business to come back to."

"Laying it on pretty thick there, aren't you, Joanne?"

"You know it's all out of love, sis. I don't want to see you get hurt, and I don't want your business to fail. We're an entrepreneurial family, and I can't see you going to get a regular job, girl."

"I know, I know." Joi had to admit her sister was right about that. They'd been raised from the cradle to think of themselves as businesswomen, never as employees. From a very young age, Joi could remember helping her mother in the boutique. She and her sister had spent hours learning to sew, keeping the store clean and even interacting with suppliers and vendors on their mother's behalf. Joanne, gifted with towering height and graceful carriage, had even modeled some of their mother's exclusive designs.

The two sisters lapsed into silence for a few minutes. Joi thought back on her upbringing, and the values their parents had instilled in them. Their mother had opened Panache back when Joanne was a baby. Her father, a high school chemistry teacher, often lamented never going into business for himself. Joi remembered her sweet sixteen party, when her parents had given her a savings bond earmarked toward the opening of her first business. *It's a lot easier to finance college than to finance a start-up,* her father had explained. That four-figure investment had later provided the down payment on the office building that now housed Citadel. Joanne had gotten a similar gift for her eighteenth birthday, and had invested it before using it to purchase the space for Wine and Whimsy.

But there was something else Emma and Tyler had passed down to Joi, perhaps without knowing it. Seeing them together, and witnessing the level of commitment and love they shared, made Joi long for a similar connection with a man. She didn't know if Marco would be that man, but there was only one way to find out.

"So, what are you going to do now? Are you really going to pursue this thing with him, despite the catastrophe it could cause?"

She looked at her sister, and could see the worry etching her face. Sometimes she felt like having Joanne in her life was like having a second mother. But since she knew how fiercely her sister loved her, she softened her expression. "Joanne, I tried. I swear I did.

But there is something between us that I can't ignore anymore. What if he's the one? Wouldn't that make it worth the risk?"

Joanne looked thoughtful, but remained quiet.

"It's ironic, when you think about it. Maybe Ernesto wasn't the one, but his friend might be."

"I don't know about this, Joi."

So she related the story of Tia Jackson and her ceramic bank full of lemonade money. When she finished, Joanne sat up straighter in her seat.

"Handsome, intelligent, charming and compassionate with children? Can all of that exist in one man?" Her brow furrowed, as if she were pondering the answer to her own question.

Joi nodded, a smile spreading across her face as she remembered Marco's interaction with little Tia. "Apparently so. I know you think it's crazy, and maybe it is. But I have to see where this could go. Don't you want me to have what Mom and Dad have? And what you have with Victor?"

Joanne's expression changed, the tense furrow of her brow releasing. "Of course I want that for you, Joi."

"Then let me go after it."

"Okay, Joi. Do what you feel is right." With a soft smile on her face, Joanne opened her arms. "Now come give me a hug."

Joi pushed her throw aside and went to sit next to her sister on the couch. They shared a tight hug, and then Joi snuggled next to Joanne's side for the rest of the movie. It was just like when they were kids, Joanne sitting there with Joi's head resting on her shoulder.

Joanne nudged her gently as she resumed the film. "Just don't say I didn't warn you."

Shaking her head, Joi turned her attention back toward the screen.

Inside the bustling interior of Bentley's on 27, Marco perused the lunch menu. Located on the twenty-seventh floor of the Charlotte Plaza building, Bentley's offered a variety of delicious French food, along with fantastic views of the Queen City skyline. He loved the food there, but his wandering mind made it difficult to decide what to order. It had been three days since the night Joi had come to him and asked to be kissed. They'd spent that time sharing discrete smiles, and sneaking away when they could to steal a few moments alone together. Despite that, he still hadn't gotten his fill of her.

Roosevelt, seated across from him in the booth, shook his head. "You still haven't decided?"

"No. Just give me a minute."

"It's already been fifteen minutes, and we do have to get back to the bank this afternoon," Roosevelt groused. "What do you have a taste for?"

Marco glanced up from his menu, feeling a wry smile lift the corners of his lips. He considered telling Roosevelt that what he really had a craving for was Joi; her lips, her smile and her powerful allure.

Roosevelt seemed to sense the direction of his thoughts, because he chuckled. "I meant, what *food* do you have a taste for? I should have been more specific."

Feigning ignorance, Marco shook his head. "I admit nothing."

Scoffing, Roosevelt took a drink from his water

glass. "You don't have to admit it. I can see what's going on between you and Ms. Lewis."

He rolled his eyes. While he considered Roosevelt a friend, they weren't close enough to be discussing this. So he used Roosevelt's impatience to his advantage, and changed the subject. "I think I'm just going to get the lobster BLT."

"Good choice. I'm getting that, too." Roosevelt raised his hand in the air, to signal for the waiter to come take their order.

Once the waiter had left with their menus, Marco sank back into the padded leather cushion of the booth seat. This morning's interaction with Joi had been brief, since she was working with her guards and technology assistant, and he'd been inundated with calls, paperwork and other duties. He wondered what she was doing now, or if she'd even taken a lunch break. Her work ethic was off the charts, and she never seemed to stop for longer than a few minutes at a time.

"You realize everyone in the bank can see what's happening, don't you?" Roosevelt leaned forward, his elbows resting on the tabletop.

Marco looked at his branch manager and shrugged. "It doesn't matter. Neither of us can deny how we feel."

"I'm not saying I don't approve, but I'm saying you need to be careful. Ms. Lewis and her staff are competent, professional and well equipped for the job."

"I agree."

"Then I'm sure you know that you shouldn't do anything to jeopardize the business relationship between Royal and Citadel." Roosevelt's gaze was steady and serious as he awaited Marco's response.

Before he could open his mouth, the waiter appeared

with their meals. As the steaming plates were set before them, the aroma of the grilled lobster and peppered bacon wafted into the air. Marco inhaled the fragrance, his stomach rumbling in anticipation. He'd been so distracted that he hadn't realized how hungry he was until the food arrived. He dug into his sandwich, wanting to get at least one bite in before he gave his rebuttal to Roosevelt's statement.

Roosevelt picked up his fork as well, and they ate for a few silent moments.

Having quelled his growling stomach, Marco paused. "Roosevelt, I understand your concern. But Joi and I are both adults, and we're perfectly capable of handling this in a mature manner."

Swallowing a mouthful, Roosevelt chuckled. "It's not Ms. Lewis I'm worried about. It's you. Your record with women isn't the best, at least not in terms of having stable relationships."

Marco didn't respond to that, because it was true. In the entirety of his life, he'd never dated any woman for longer than three months. No woman had ever held his attention at a high enough level to justify it. However, things were already very different with Joi. She was unique, unlike any of the women he'd encountered in the past.

"You're not disputing me. Makes sense. We both know you don't have a leg to stand on."

"This isn't just a fling, Roosevelt. There's something special between us."

Roosevelt didn't look convinced. "We'll see. Just don't screw it up, because I really think Citadel is the best fit for the security contract. We'd be hard-pressed to find another contractor this good."

"I agree, and you have nothing to worry about." Marco went back to eating, hoping Roosevelt would take the hint and end the conversation. After all, as the branch manager had pointed out, they did have to return to the bank for the afternoon shift.

"One more thing. You realize tomorrow is inventory day, right?"

Marco stopped midchew. He'd completely forgotten about the inventory, which had been scheduled months prior, during the tenure of their previous security contractor. This was a physical inventory, which involved the branch president and the security chief taking a count, by hand, of everything contained in the branch's safe deposit boxes. *That means...*

"Yep. That means you and Ms. Lewis will be spending most of the day in the vault." Roosevelt gave voice to his thoughts. "Think you can handle it?"

They both knew he didn't have a choice, because company protocol dictated that no one could stand in for the president, or the security chief, unless one of them had extenuating circumstances. "Of course I can handle it."

And he could. He would let Joi dictate the tone of things, because he had too much respect for her to put her in a situation she didn't approve of. If she were in any way uncomfortable with the idea of being alone in the vault with him, she could invite one of her guards to join them. The work would be completed either way, because he was first and foremost a professional. "Did you let Joi know about the inventory?"

Roosevelt shook his head. "No, but I will this afternoon."

He nodded, wondering how she would react to the

news. As he finished up his lunch, he decided not to worry about it, because he would know the answer soon enough. Gesturing to the waiter for the check, he lifted his hips from the seat to retrieve his wallet.

In the past, he'd found the inventories dull and tedious, but he didn't think that would be an issue this time.

He had a very distinct feeling this inventory would be intriguing, to say the least.

Chapter 10

It was just after eight on Friday morning, and a few early birds were already inside the bank. As Joi exited the break room, she watched the bank's customers coming and going, filling in deposit slips, sitting in the waiting area or doing business at the teller desk. She knew she should be walking down the hallway toward the vault, but she stood there for a few moments, hoping to gather herself for today's task.

When Roosevelt had informed her the previous day of the inventory she'd be expected to participate in, she'd been a little stunned. As a security expert, she understood why the inventory was a necessary function for the bank, and why two people were assigned to perform it instead of one person alone. Still, as things stood between her and Marco, she predicted a very charged environment within the confines of the vault.

Jackie strolled through the open double doors leading to the corridor, walking up to Joi.

"Morning, Jackie."

"Morning, boss lady. What's the matter with you? Your face is mighty tight."

Joi sighed. "I'm on inventory duty today with Mr. Alvarez. I anticipate the day will be very tedious and dull." It was the best excuse she could think of to explain her sour expression. She certainly wasn't about to tell her guard the real reason.

Jackie's expression morphed into a knowing smile. "I don't think so. Not since you and Mr. Alvarez are obviously smitten with each other."

Joi said nothing, choosing instead to fix Jackie with a censuring look.

She waved her off. "Don't give me that look. You don't have to admit it, I already know the deal." She moved on down the hall, toward her duty station outside the vault door.

With a groan, Joi followed her. The last thing she needed right now was for her guards and the bank staff to be gossiping about the chemistry between her and Marco. Her attraction to Marco was impractical, inconvenient and probably ill-advised. It was also very real, and so far she hadn't been able to push it away.

She was standing by the vault door with Jackie when Marco strode out of his office, which faced the vault. He looked quite dashing in a black suit, crisp white shirt and black-white-and-yellow-patterned tie. He pulled a small wheeled cart along behind him.

"Good morning, ladies." While Marco's greeting encompassed the both of them, the smile he wore seemed to be directed at Joi.

Jackie nodded a greeting in return.

"Good morning, Marco." Joi took a small step out of the way, so he could approach the vault. "Is there anything I should bring in with me for the inventory?"

He shook his head. "No. I have all the necessary supplies with me." He gestured to his cart.

"Okay, sounds good." Inside, she was both nervous and giddy, but she refused to let on. What mattered most to her was that he saw her as a professional; someone capable of handling any task they might be assigned.

She watched him input a series of codes into the keypad on the vault door. A long beep and a flashing green light emitted from the keypad, and then he spun the handle on the vault door and pulled it open. The big door took a few tugs to release, and then he opened it about halfway.

He turned back toward her, and spoke. "Joi, I know the inventory came as a surprise to you, and I apologize that you weren't given more notice."

She kept her expression blank. "It's not a problem."

"I'm glad to hear that." His appearance turned more serious. "I want to make sure you're comfortable with completing the inventory with me."

"I am."

"Because if you're not, I'd be glad to allow your guard to accompany us inside the vault, or whatever would work best for you."

Aware of Jackie's listening ears, Joi kept her voice even. "Marco, I'm fine with carrying out the inventory according to the bank's rules. You don't need to make any special arrangements for me." In her mind, she knew that meant she was agreeing to be alone inside the vault with Marco for an undisclosed period of time. She told herself that it didn't matter, that she was simply here to perform a job. But her heart knew that the time alone with him was bound to bring her feelings to the surface.

"All right. And remember, if at any time you change your mind, we'll stop the inventory and make adjustments." Marco had already slipped inside the brightly lit interior of the vault.

With a brief glance toward her grinning guard, Joi followed Marco into the vault. The chill hanging in the air was the first thing she noticed, and it made her close the open halves of her blazer, and button it. Apparently the vault wasn't heated, at least not as much as the rest of the bank's interior.

Marco instructed Jackie, "Leave the door just slightly ajar, please. That way if there's an emergency we can be heard."

"Yes, sir." Jackie tugged on the vault door, leaving a thin sliver of space between the door and the frame.

When Joi turned Marco's way, she saw him stooped down, taking things out of the small cart he'd brought in with him. She watched as he opened up a small tray table, setting it up in the center of the room. On it he placed four bottles of water, an electronic scanner and a small basket of snacks.

"I see you've thought of everything." She walked over to get a closer look at the contents of the basket. It held a few apples and bananas, protein bars and a jar of mixed nuts.

He smiled. "I've done the inventory twice before, and after I learned how long it could take, I realized it made sense to be extra prepared."

"How long is it going to take?"

"Two and a half to three hours. Sometimes it seems longer, with the vault being so chilly."

She pointed to the black scanner device next to the basket. "I'm assuming this is your inventory gun?"

"Yes." He picked it up and turned it on. "The device takes a photograph of everything we count, and I use this keypad to enter data to go along with each photo."

"And what's my role as security chief?"

"To go behind me with your own gun." He produced another device from the cart, handing it to her. "If our records aren't an exact match, that's an indication of a problem. There's also a paper document to be filled in, but Roosevelt will take care of that."

"Show me how this works. I don't want to get it wrong."

He powered her device on, and gave her a brief tutorial on how to operate it. Then he asked, "Do you feel comfortable enough with it to get started?"

She nodded.

"Do you feel comfortable enough with me? Because my promise remains intact, Joi."

She drew in a deep breath. "I'm fine, Marco."

A ghost of a smile crossed his handsome face. "Then let's get started."

Starting in one corner of the vault, the two of them moved around the perimeter of the room to perform the inventory. Marco used his skeleton key to open each box, used the machine to record the data and then stepped back so Joi could mimic his steps. At box number twenty-eight, the transition between his steps and hers happened a bit too fast, with her stepping up to the box before he had a chance to back away. The back of her body was in full contact with the front of his for a few seconds, and the heat of his nearness seeped right through the fabric barriers between them. A tingle ran down her spine, and she deeply inhaled the cool air scented with his cologne. Once she got her bearings again, she hazarded a glance at him. His expression showed no signs that he'd been uncomfortable with the contact, but when he winked at her, she had to turn away.

Touching him made her feel reckless, uninhibited. They'd managed to get most of the job done with very little physical contact, but when it came to Marco, it didn't take much. As she tried to turn her attention back to the work at hand, Joi knew that if they touched again, she would probably give in to every lusty urge she harbored for him.

As they reached the midpoint at the seventy-fifth box, Marco asked, "Do you need a break?"

"Yes. My eyes are starting to cross from looking at the screen on this thing." She gestured to her inventory gun.

He moved toward the center of the room, near the table, and set his machine down.

Joi followed suit.

He observed her, noting that she appeared to be watching his every move. Cracking open the cap on a bottle of water, he held it out to her. "Here you go. And have a snack if you'd like."

She reached out for the water, and their hands touched.

He felt the familiar crackle of electricity run through his body. The one he felt every time they touched.

Taking the water from him, she drank a long sip before setting it aside. Her gaze never left his face.

Curious about her state of mind, he asked, "Are you all right, Joi?"

She recapped the water bottle and set it down. Her tongue darted out to lick a few stray droplets of water from her glossy lips. "I will be, once you kiss me."

His body reacted to the heat in her words and in her gaze. Mentally willing his erection to stand down, he spoke softly. "Are you sure? We still have quite a bit of work to do."

"It will get done, don't worry. But right now all I can think about is this." She eased closer to him, and when she entered his personal space, her fingertips rose to graze over the line of his jaw.

The temperature in the vault seemed to rise twenty degrees in that moment. He crooked his finger, then placed it beneath her chin to tilt her face up, at just the right angle. Then he leaned in, letting his lips brush against hers.

The kiss was at first pensive; sweet and fleeting. Soon, the rising heat of desire spurred him on, and he deepened the kiss. As his tongue swept between her lips, she grasped either side of his face while he draped his arms around her waist. He drew her as close to his body as he could, savoring both the sweetness of her mouth and the feel of her feminine softness pressed against him. A soft murmur escaped her throat, muffled by the seal of their lips, and his manhood tightened again.

He knew that if they kept this up, they would end up in a position that might compromise the overall great working atmosphere at the bank. Reluctantly, he ended the kiss.

A guilty look flashed over Joi's countenance, and she let her hands drop away, releasing her hold on his face.

For a few moments, only the sounds of their rapid breathing filled the space.

His arms were still draped around her waist. Looking into the crystalline pools of her dark eyes, he offered a slight smile. "I don't know about you, but I'm not cold anymore."

She blushed, and he found the color filling her cheeks both amusing and endearing.

"It's time I took you on a proper date, Joi. Come to my band's show tonight, and I'll take you out afterward."

Her expression turned sly. "And what will we do after that?"

He shrugged. "I'll let you lead, and we'll see where the night takes us. So will you come?"

Appearing pleased, she nodded. "Just tell me the time and place."

He filled her in on the details of the show, and after they each had a piece of fruit and a protein bar, the inventory continued.

Seated on the stage with his saxophone lying across his lap, Marco looked at the blue velvet curtain in front of him. From the other side, he could hear the boisterous cheers of the Friday-night crowd at the Blue Lounge, as they awaited the beginning of the Queen City Gents show. His bandmates were set up around him, each man readying his instrument for the performance, which would begin at any moment. The four of them took a great deal of pride in putting on an entertaining show. Tonight, Marco knew that his greatest concern would be the opinion of one audience member in particular: Joi.

The heated moments they'd shared in the bank vault earlier that day had spurred him on toward asking her to attend a Gents show. Not only would it give her a chance to see him in action on the sax, but he also planned to take her to the best dessert spot in the city. Once they were alone, he planned to show her his "sweeter" side, and he genuinely hoped she'd enjoy herself with him.

The owner of the lounge announced the band, and Marco watched as the curtain rose to reveal the faces of the people in attendance at the show. It was a packed house, as it usually was on weekends. The front tables were again filled with female fans, who'd paid extra to sit close to the stage. His gaze quickly zeroed in on Joi, who was sitting at one of those tables, just to the left of center stage. She looked gorgeous, with her hair sleekly styled, and a close-fitting sweater and skirt hugging the curves of her frame. Her legs were encased in a pair of thigh-high boots with stiletto heels, and she sat with them crossed demurely in front of her. Not wanting to miss his cue, he dragged his eyes away from her and focused on Rashad, who functioned as vocalist, pianist and bandleader during their shows.

Rashad, seated on a bench in front of the upright piano, raised his hand high. Ken tapped out a count with his sticks, and the Gents eased into their first number, the Charlie Parker classic, "Bird of Paradise."

As Marco carried the melody on his saxophone,

he glanced back and forth between the sheet music and Joi. Since he knew the composition by heart, his wandering eye didn't affect his performance. Seeing Joi swaying in her seat made him glad the band had decided to lead the set with a song that showcased his talents on the sax. A few women had risen from their seats to hang out near the edge of the stage, and for the first time, Marco didn't even bother to look their way. He only had eyes for Joi.

When the set ended, he rushed to get his instrument packed away so he could whisk her off to their next destination.

As he jogged toward the stage door that led to the main area of the lounge, with his sax case in hand, he darted by Ken.

"Where are you hurrying off to?"

"Got a date. Later, man." And he didn't hang around to continue the conversation.

He entered into the main area of the lounge, and stopped short when he saw a smiling Joi conversing with a tall, fair-skinned man. A twinge of jealousy tightened his face, but he held off on saying anything so they could finish their conversation.

Noticing him, Joi waved him over. "Marco, there you are. This is Trevor. We went to high school together. Trevor, this is Marco, my date."

Hearing her refer to him as her "date" helped ease the tension building inside him. He stuck out his hand to the man towering over him. "Nice to meet you, Trevor."

"Likewise." Trevor shook Marco's hand, then returned his attention to Joi. "I won't hold you up from your date, but it was nice seeing you again."

"Nice seeing you, too." She waved as Trevor departed, then turned back to him. "Ready to go?"

"Let's go." Offering his arm, he guided her past the stage and out the side door. They paused for a moment to shrug into their coats, then he swung open the door and they stepped out into the clear, cold night.

He slipped his hand over hers as they walked. At his sedan, he popped the trunk with the remote on his key and placed his saxophone case inside. Snapping the trunk shut, he grasped her hand again and continued to walk.

Her confusion apparent, she asked, "We're not taking the car?" He'd picked her up from home earlier in the evening, and she didn't look very enthusiastic about walking in the chilly weather.

"No. The place I'm taking you to is less than a block away." He could see the wisps of frozen vapor coming from their mouths, and vowed to get her out of this cold as quickly as he could.

She nodded, letting him lead her down the lamp-lit sidewalk.

Chapter 11

They came to a stop in front of Frosting and Sprinkles, and he grasped the door handle with his free hand. "Here we are."

A smile spread across Joi's face. "How did you know I have a sweet tooth?"

"Lucky guess. Let's get inside out of this cold."

Inside the warm confines of the shop, the air was scented with the aromas of baked sweets: cookies, cakes and various pastries. The walls were painted a soft aqua shade, and framed drawings of baked goods adorned the walls. There were a few booths in the corners of the space, but the center of the shop was filled with small, round iron tables and matching scrollwork chairs, perfectly sized for two people.

There were no other customers in the place, and Joi liked the idea of the privacy that would provide them.

The female baker, clad in a snow-white apron, grinned as he approached. "Good to see you again, Mr. Alvarez. Your order's just about to come out of the oven."

"Perfect timing, Kelly. Please meet Joi." He approached the counter, still grasping her hand.

Kelly nodded to her as she slipped on a pair of oven mitts. "Welcome, Joi. I think you're really going to love this." Sidling over to the oven, she opened it.

Joi inhaled the rich aroma of apples and cinnamon that filled the air, her stomach rumbling in anticipation. "Oh my gosh, what is that heavenly smell?"

The baker pulled out two ceramic ramekins, setting them carefully on the counter near the stove. "My vanilla apple crisp. The house specialty."

Joi watched with round eyes as Kelly topped the two steaming bowls with a healthy dollop of vanilla ice cream, then a ribbon of what looked like butterscotch or caramel sauce. Setting the twin desserts on a tray, she added two gleaming silver spoons, then brought the tray over to Marco. "Here you go."

Marco smiled as he accepted it. "Thanks, Kelly. These look great."

"Enjoy." Kelly winked, and disappeared into the kitchen area.

He carried the tray to a booth in the corner, and she trailed a few steps behind him. He stepped back to allow her to sit down first. She settled into the soft cushioned seat. Moments later, she was both surprised and delighted when he chose to sit next to her instead of taking the bench across the table.

His eyes met hers. "Is it all right if I sit next to you?"

She felt the involuntary flutter of her lashes as she answered him. "By all means, join me."

"Good, because after watching you all night from the stage, I want to be as close to you as possible." He picked up one of the spoons and stuck it into one of the desserts.

A shiver of anticipation ran down her spine. She sensed a pleasurable experience coming on, and not just from the sweet concoction he spooned up.

She was about to dig into the other crisp when she noticed he hadn't eaten the spoonful he had.

Instead, he guided the spoon toward her mouth. His dark eyes dancing with desire, he cajoled her. "Open up, Joi."

The sensual double meaning of his words touched her very core, and she licked her lips before parting them as he'd asked.

The moment she tasted the mingled flavors of the tender apples and flaky crust, accented by vanilla and cinnamon, she groaned aloud.

His thick brows rose a few inches. "That's the sound of pleasure if I ever heard it. I'm happy to be the one to cause it."

Her face flushed with heat, she angled her gaze away from him. After she'd chewed and swallowed the first mouthful of crisp, she sighed. "This is *so* good."

That remark drew a deep, rumbling chuckle from him. "It's my favorite thing here. I'm glad you like it."

"Less talking, more feeding." She opened her mouth again.

He looked downright amused. Shaking his head, he fed her another spoonful, then another. "If I'm going to feed you, you'll have to do the same so I can have some."

"Fair enough." She picked up the other spoon, and acted accordingly.

They continued that way, feeding each other in turn, until the two ramekins were empty.

Using her index finger to swipe up the last bit of melted ice cream in one of the dishes, Joi stuck the tip in her mouth and sucked it gently. It wasn't until she'd already made the gesture that she realized how it must look to Marco. When she swung her gaze his way, she found his eyes locked on her lips, where her finger still rested.

Embarrassment rose within her, and she drew her hand away from her mouth. "Sorry. It was so good I forgot myself."

His intense gaze remained on her lips as he spoke. "Don't apologize for enjoying yourself, Joi. That's why I brought you here." He eased closer to her on the seat, until their thighs were touching. "Forgive me for being so forward, but I'd love to give you further enjoyment."

Seeing the flames of desire igniting his gaze emboldened her, and she slipped her arm around his shoulder. "And I'd love to experience what you have to offer, Marco."

He used his fingertips to angle her face, then pressed his lips to hers. The kiss was filled with yearning, and the unspoken craving they had for each other. When he eased away, she felt breathless and dazed. She could have sworn she saw stars.

He slid out of the booth and stood. After he reached into his pocket and pulled out a twenty-dollar bill to lay on the table, he reached out for her hand. "Where to?"

She let him help her to her feet, then slung her purse over her shoulder. "Your place."

"As you wish." Still grasping her hand, he led her out of the bakery.

Outside in the chilly night air, they jogged back to the Blue Lounge, where his car remained parked in the lot. The two of them climbed in and buckled up, and he started the engine. As a wonderful warmth began to radiate from the seat to chase away the chill, she sighed.

"Heated seats," she stated softly, while sinking into the buttery soft leather.

"Are there any other kind?" He guided the car down the road with one hand, laying the other hand atop her thigh.

The warmth of his touch rivaled the heat generated by the seats, and she felt her core shudder in anticipation of the special brand of "enjoyment" he planned to provide her once they reached his house.

The twenty-minute drive was filled with heated glances, stolen kisses and possessive squeezes of her thigh, and by the time he pulled his car into the garage adjoining his large Tudor-style home, she could feel the liquid warmth pooling in her panties.

When he opened the passenger door to help her out of the car, she found her legs a bit shaky. He steadied her with a sure arm around her waist as he used his free hand to close the garage door via remote. With that done, he walked her up the three stone steps to the door, unlocked it and ushered her inside.

Automatic recessed lights activated, illuminating his gourmet kitchen. While he removed his coat, she had just a few moments to admire the gleaming stainless steel appliances and beige-hued stone countertops before he whisked her into his arms.

"I have another dessert in mind, one even sweeter than the apple crisp."

She smiled. "My… Looks like you have an even bigger sweet tooth than I do."

He started to back up, still holding her. As he moved the two of them across the room, he kept her occupied with hot kisses placed against her lips, jaw, cheeks and forehead. Her eyes slid closed as she gave herself over to the sensations he evoked. He drew her arms out of her pea coat, tossing it aside. She was so dazzled she didn't notice what he was doing until he turned her around and gently pressed her hips down onto a firm, hard surface.

She opened her eyes then, to ascertain her location. A brief glance at her surroundings revealed her to be sitting on top of a very expensive-looking table in his breakfast nook. The table occupied a small alcove in the kitchen, surrounded by floor-to-ceiling windows. The amber-colored drapes were drawn shut against the darkness outside.

For a moment, she felt confused. Confusion gave way to wonder when he speared his hands through her hair and drew her in for a kiss that left her panting.

She offered up no resistance as he lifted her gray sweater up.

"Can I?" His words were throaty, his breathing labored.

"Yes…" There was no other response to his masterful teasing, at least not one she wanted to give.

She raised her arms, letting him remove her sweater and camisole. His lips blazed a trail along the top edge of her lacy bra, the heady sensations making her head loll back. In that moment, she knew she would gladly let him do whatever he wished, because she didn't want the pleasure to end.

But as she watched him pull out a chair and take a seat squarely in front of her partially open legs, her breath caught in her throat. She'd forgone tights or pantyhose due to the height of her leather boots, which encased most of her legs. She watched with hooded eyes as he slid his hands up her thighs.

"Rise up for me, sweetheart."

She did as he asked, and as she lifted her hips from the tabletop, he dragged her panties down her legs, carefully easing them off around her boots.

She started to inquire if he was going to remove them, but as he hiked up her wool pencil skirt and leaned forward, she knew he had no interest in her footwear.

In the next heartbeat, her boots were draped over his back.

As Marco let his fingertips play over Joi's most secret place, he inhaled her intoxicating natural scent. Her arousal was easy to detect. Even in the dim light he could see the evidence as she lay splayed out atop his table. He was already steel hard, but he'd promised her enjoyment, and tonight he would give her as much as she could stand. Even if she decided to retreat again behind her barrier of professionalism, he wanted her to always remember this night, and what they'd shared.

A smile touched his lips as he prepared to feast on the most decadent dessert a man could partake of.

His tongue darted out, giving her a slow, deliberate

lick. That first contact from his mouth tore a strangled cry from her lips. Easing back, he asked, "Would you like me to stop?"

"Don't you dare," came the breathless reply. With her fingertips speared through his hair, she drew him back in.

He did as she demanded, lingering between her open thighs with her boot-encased legs draped over his shoulders. She was sweet, even more so than he could have imagined. The more he licked, kissed and teased her core, the more her hips rose from the table. Her back arched, and her melodious moans filled his kitchen with the loveliest sound he'd ever heard. His erection lengthened and stretched in response to her. Soon his ministrations overwhelmed her, and she screamed his name on the wings of an orgasm, her body trembling with the force of it.

He slid the chair back, and took in the sight of her in the afterglow of her enjoyment. The tableau she made, writhing sensuously atop his table, was even more beautiful than a Costa Rican sunset over the cerulean waters of the Caribbean Sea. "You are beautiful," he said aloud, giving voice to his thoughts.

"Ahh." It appeared a moan was all she could manage.

He helped her sit up, then gathered her into his arms. As he carried her toward the steps, he whispered in her ear. "The next time, I'll spread a little honey there, and over your nipples, and devour you like the delicacy you are."

Another moan escaped her, and her head dropped against his shoulder.

He brought her onto the second level of the house,

and into his bedroom. Lying her atop the comforter on his king-size bed, he stripped off his clothes.

He heard her say something, but couldn't understand her. She'd turned her face into the pillows, and the move had effectively muffled her voice.

"What did you say, Dulce?"

"I said, hurry."

Knowing she yearned for him boosted his male pride. Not one to disappoint a beautiful woman, he made haste in getting undressed and retrieving protection from the drawer in his nightstand. Bringing the small packet with him, he joined her on the bed, fully nude.

She sat up, seeming somewhat recovered from her first release. Her gaze beckoned to him, as did her index finger.

He reached around her to unhook her bra, tossing the garment aside. The weight of her breasts fell free, and he spent time suckling the hardened tip of each dark nipple. When he had her breathless and panting to his liking, he knelt on the floor and unzipped each tall boot, removing them in turn. Then he dragged the skirt away from her, drinking in the erotic sight of her nudity. The lush curves of her body called to him, so he took a moment to run his hands over each peak and valley. Only when he deemed her thoroughly ready for him did he cease, so he could roll on the condom.

Once he'd sheathed himself with the protection, he adjusted her on her back in the center of his bed. "Are you comfortable, Dulce?"

She nodded, reaching out for him.

As they embraced, she parted her thighs for him.

While his lips crushed against hers, he angled his hips and entered her slowly.

Her hands drifted down to his waist, drawing him in until he'd entered her fully. The warm tightness of her body sheltering his felt heavenly, and as he began to stroke, the sensation of ecstasy only increased.

Her soft, throaty cries mingled with his groans as he made love to her. Her eyes were closed, and her head moved back and forth over the wealth of pillows supporting her. Her legs wound around his waist, spurring him to lengthen his thrusts. He followed the cues she gave him in altering his strokes to her liking, all the while doing his best to hold back the orgasm he felt building inside. He wanted to make her come again, wanted to feel her inner muscles flex around him.

Fate chose to grant his wish, because in the next breath, her shouts of joy echoed inside his bedroom. He knew she was coming because he could feel her body spasm, capturing him in the most sensual grip. Before long, his own orgasm roared through his body, and he growled at the behest of the magic radiating through him.

He withdrew from her, and left her briefly to dispose of the condom. When he returned, she lay on her side with her back to him. His eyes rested on the lush curve of her backside as he approached. The closer he got, the easier it became for him to hear her light snores ruffling the silence.

With gentle hands, he shifted her around until he could get her beneath the covers. She barely noticed as he pulled the sheets and comforter up over her. When he thought she looked comfortable, he lifted the corner of the bedclothes and slid in next to her, his body pressed against hers in a spoon position. Draping his arm over her, he pulled her close. Still sound asleep, she snuggled into him.

He intended to go to sleep himself, but he found he couldn't close his eyes. All he could do was stare at her, looking so peaceful and at home in his bed, and in his arms. His heart turned over in his chest, and he knew that if she changed her mind about being with him, he would be lost. As much as he dreaded where it might lead, he knew he was developing very serious feelings for her. He wouldn't exactly define what he felt as love, but whatever it was, it was possessive. He didn't want any other man looking at her, much less holding her this way.

As he watched her sleep, he tried to tell himself that he was still in control, even though he knew it was a lie. She now held immeasurable power over him, and he saw no way to shift that dynamic. If she walked away from him now, after what they'd shared, getting over her would be next to impossible.

Chapter 12

When Joi entered the bank Monday morning, she found herself looking around the interior with new eyes. She knew that nothing had changed there, but plenty had changed inside her. A smile spread across her face as she thought of Marco, who she assumed was in his office by now. She cheerily greeted her guards and the bank staff as she made her way through the double doors in the glass wall separating the office corridor from the main customer area of the bank.

She couldn't remember when she'd had a more fantastic weekend. She'd awoken in Marco's arms Saturday morning, and they'd spent part of the day at a local bookstore, perusing the record section. She'd left with a copy of *The Very Best of John Coltrane* on vinyl, and he'd dropped her off at home. She'd then passed the rest of the weekend enjoying her new album and catching up on the stack of books she'd been intending to read for the past several months. Today, she felt renewed, refreshed and a little bit like a schoolgirl who'd landed a date with her crush.

When she rounded the corner past the vault, she saw him leaning against the frame of his office door. He was dressed in yet another well-cut suit, this one in a shade of beige. Beneath the sport coat he wore a royal blue shirt and a blue-and-white-striped tie. He had an open newspaper in his hands, and wore a pair of black-framed reading glasses that somehow made him look even more dashing.

"Good morning, Marco." She felt her body temperature rising as she entered his space.

He placed a fleeting kiss against her temple. "Good morning, Dulce."

She could feel the heat rushing to her cheeks. "I thought we agreed you wouldn't call me that here at work."

"My apologies. Your beauty made me forget my oath." He grasped her hand, lifted it to his lips and kissed the back of it.

A soft giggle caught their attention.

Both Joi and Marco turned their focus toward the vault, where Jackie had just taken her assigned post. Amusement was clearly written on the guard's face.

Joi gave Jackie a stern look, to which Jackie responded, "Carry on, you two."

Marco chuckled. "I'm tempted to do just that, but then no work would get done around here."

Knowing he was right, Joi edged away from him. "I'm going back up front with Yolanda. I just wanted to come see you for a minute."

"Have a good day, Du… I mean, Joi." He tipped an imaginary hat in her direction.

Sighing, she turned around and went back the way she'd come.

A couple hours later, Joi was standing with Yolanda in the waiting area, going over Yolanda's request for time off. A sudden long, shrill beeping sound cut through the conversations of the bank's patrons, and both Joi and Yolanda turned toward the teller's desk, where the noise was coming from.

Nancy, the lead teller, had hopped down from her stool and was now staring at her computer screen in bewilderment. "Something's wrong. The computer won't let me pull up any account data!" She had to shout to be heard over the sound.

Joi rushed over to the desk, with her phone in hand. Dashing off a text message to Chloe, Karen's tech assistant.

One by one, the other two teller computer terminals shut down, and began making the same loud, obnoxious sound as Nancy's machine. Joi didn't have a clue what was going on, but whatever happened, she knew she had to stop that sound, because she was starting to get a headache.

Apparently, the customers in the building agreed with her, because the ones who hadn't already left the premises now had their hands placed over their ears.

Yolanda ran over, ducking behind the teller desk. With a quick yank, she disconnected the power strips, which immediately powered off the teller's machines. Thankfully, the awful beeping ceased.

Roosevelt came out of his office, and was met by Marco as he approached the teller desk.

Marco asked, "What's going on out here?" He waved the staff over, and soon they were all standing in a tight circle near the desk.

Nancy, who looked wholly nervous, replied, "I'm not sure, but something's wrong with the computer system."

"Yeah. It kicked us all off our terminals," another teller added.

"My computer went down, too!" This came from the loan officer, who'd stuck her head out of her office door to make the announcement. It occurred to Joi that this was the first good look she'd gotten at her, since she rarely came out of her office.

Marco turned his eyes to Joi. "Has anyone tried to use the ATMs outside?"

Joi shook her head. "I don't think so."

"I'll go." Jackie strode out the front door.

For a few minutes, everyone milled about, waiting for Jackie to return with news.

When she did, the news was not good. "The ATMs are down, too. Nothing but a blank blue screen on both of them."

Roosevelt cursed. "Sorry, but a blue screen is never a good sign for a computer." Shoving his hands into his pockets, he directed his next statement at Marco. "I think we've got some kind of electronic security breach going on."

This time, Marco cursed. "We've gone dark, so we need to get the customers out of here. Without the computer system, we can't service any of their accounts."

Joi dispatched Yolanda and Jackie to escort the few remaining customers outside, and Marco sent his tellers and loan officer home for the day. Some of the customers were not pleased with being sent away from the bank without having their requests fulfilled, and they made their displeasure known. Marco reacted with practiced patience, promising the frustrated patrons restitution for their inconvenience. Once the group was reduced to just the remaining bank staff, Marco strode over to lock the doors.

Before he could turn the latch, Chloe came running up. Marco opened the door and let her in, then locked it as he'd intended.

Chloe ran up to Joi, and said breathlessly, "I got here as fast as I could. I had a ten o'clock class."

Joi placed a hand on the young woman's shoulder. "I'm glad you're here. How much experience do you have with Karen's cybersecurity software?" She knew that her partner used a proprietary software that encrypted and protected their customer's data. Karen had built the program herself, from the ground up, and all the businesses that Citadel serviced used it. That made Joi wonder if any of her other clients were experiencing problems, but she knew she had to deal with what was in front of her before she could investigate.

Chloe's expression turned sheepish. "Not much. She'd just started training me on it before she took that fall, and we'd only gotten up to module seven."

Joi felt her brow crease. "How many modules are there?"

"Twenty." Chloe answered the question in a soft voice, as if she hoped that would make it easier to hear.

It didn't. Joi pressed her open palm to her face. "Holy crap. I have to get Karen on the phone." She strode to the corridor, phone in hand, dialing her partner's number as she walked.

"Hello?" Gabe's voice came on the line.

"Hey, Gabe. Let me speak to Karen."

"I can't. She just had a dose of the meds they prescribed her for pain, and she's already passed out."

Joi pressed her fingers to her temple. "How long will she be out?"

Gabe's voice held uncertainty. "Three, maybe four hours, at least. When she took them yesterday afternoon, she was out from dinnertime until sunrise."

There was nothing else she could say, so she asked, "Can you have her call me when she wakes up?"

"Sure thing. The moment she's coherent, she'll call."

"Thanks, Gabe." Disconnecting the call, Joi stuck the phone back into the pocket of her blazer.

How in the hell am I going to fix this mess?

Marco watched Joi through the glass wall bordering the office corridor. He could see her pacing back and forth as she made her call. Nothing about her facial expressions made him think she was getting good results from it. Turning back to Roosevelt, he met his branch manager's gaze. "Roosevelt, hang a sign on the door that says we're closed until further notice. Make sure to include our apologies for the inconvenience."

Roosevelt nodded, his expression grim. "How long do you think we'll be shut down?"

Having no answer to that, he shrugged. "Who knows? But this looks like a serious security breach, and I don't want to endanger the funds of any new depositors." Beyond that, he knew that having customers in the bank would only complicate things as he and his staff tried to sort through this mess. They would undoubtedly have questions, and right now, no one at Royal had any answers for them.

"Got it." The branch manager drifted away toward his office.

Marco spoke to Yolanda, the guard Joi had assigned to the front door. "Can you still access the security footage, even though the computer system is down?"

Yolanda produced a seven-inch tablet from the inside of her Citadel Security logo jacket. "Yes, sir. The security feed is automatically backed up to the cloud, and fully accessible from our Citadel tablets. What do you need me to do?"

"Take a look at the footage from last week, and see if you notice anything suspicious. Maybe someone came in with a flash drive, or a memory card, or someone who lingered by the ATM or made contact with any of the teller terminals. Then let me know what you find."

"I'm on it." Yolanda went to the lobby waiting area and sat down with the tablet on her lap.

He glanced at Joi again, who was now conversing in hushed tones with the tech assistant. Not knowing what solution they might come up with, or how long it would take, Marco tore his eyes away and trudged to his office. Thankfully, he also had a tablet, equipped with data service from his cell phone company. Powering on the tablet, he took a seat at his desk and put in a video call to Sal. It was the last thing he wanted to do, but he knew it was necessary to get the corporate office involved. After all, he had no way of knowing how far the security breach might extend. Was it just affecting the branch in Charlotte, or had it affected other branches worldwide?

When Sal's face came on the screen, wearing an easy smile, Marco hated to be the one to ruin his friend and boss's good mood.

"Hello, Marco. To what do I owe the pleasure, my friend?"

Marco sighed. "It's not good, Sal. I think we have a security breach."

Sal's expression immediately changed, his brow furrowing. "What? I've heard only good things about your security contractor from the branch manager."

"And I agree with Roosevelt's assessment. All our physical funds and safe deposit items are secure. The breach is electronic, and it's shut down our entire computer network."

"When did this happen?"

"Today, just under an hour ago. All the teller terminals and automated teller machines shut down. I had to close the branch."

"And your security contractor? What actions have they taken?"

"Ms. Lewis and her technologist are working on the problem as we speak, but it may take some time." He chose not to regale Sal with the details of Joi's partner being out on medical leave, or of the hapless but determined young assistant who now stood between the Charlotte branch and possible financial ruin.

By now Sal wore a deep frown. "This is terrible. Have you been in contact with any of the other branches?" Royal had branches in Manhattan, Los Angeles, Paris and London.

He shook his head. "No, Sal. I came straight to you."

Sal scratched at his bearded chin. "I suppose the first course of action is to put out a call to the other branches, to make sure there's been no ill effect to their systems. The team here can get that done in the next hour or so."

"What actions would you like us to take at the Charlotte branch?"

"Didn't you tell me that the cybersecurity software Citadel uses is proprietary?"

"It is. It's the creation of Citadel's head technologist."

Sal remained silent for a few moments, his expression becoming reflective. "Honestly, Marco, I think the best course of action is for you and Ms. Lewis, along with her technologist, to come here to Limón. Bring them to headquarters, and let them collaborate with our techs to solve the problem."

"Do you want to do that even if the breach is isolated to our branch?"

"Yes. The Charlotte branch serves a very lucrative market for us, and I don't want to risk having it collapse because of this. So I'll need you and the security team on the first plane to Limón."

"Understood. I'll make the arrangements right away."

"Good." Some of the tension seemed to drain away from Sal's face. "Text me the details of your flight, and I'll have a car pick you up from the airport."

"Thanks." Marco disconnected the video call, and placed the tablet flat on his desk. Swiveling his chair until he faced the frosted window behind the desk, he groaned. He hadn't explained the whole situation to Sal, and he felt somewhat guilty about it. Now he'd have to explain Karen's absence when he and Joi showed up with an assistant instead of Citadel's lead tech expert.

If nothing else, though, this impromptu trip to Limón to solve the breach would provide him an opportunity to escape the abnormally frigid North Carolina winter in favor of the balmy climate of his hometown. He hadn't visited home in nearly two years, and he knew his parents would be thrilled to see him. His mother would lecture him about the long stretches between his trips, but since she did that over the phone at every opportunity, he'd become accustomed to it. The real killer was her constant demand that he settle down and gift her with grandchildren.

There was also the matter of the Herreras' party. He'd already committed to it, and would now be arriving in town even sooner than he'd anticipated. In a way, Sal's edict gave him an opportunity he never thought he'd have: to take Joi as his date for the Herrera affair. The complexities of that idea were many. Most important, he had no idea how Ernesto and his parents would react to seeing the woman who'd abandoned Ernesto at the altar as Marco's date.

Thinking about the challenges the next several days would present was starting to give him a headache. So rather than dwell on them any longer, he used the tablet to access the website of his favorite airline, and initiated a search for flights that could get him to Limón within the next seventy-two hours.

Due to the lead technologist's injury, he'd have to take the assistant along. The branch would have to remain closed while the problem was resolved, but customers could still use ATMs to deposit and withdraw their money, without a fee.

He just hoped Joi's passport was in order, because they had a flight to catch.

Chapter 13

As Joi walked up the Jetway into Juan Santamaría International Airport, she couldn't remember the last time she'd been so glad to be on solid ground. She hated flying, and only did it when ground transportation was unavailable or impractical. Still, per her mother's advice, she kept her passport updated, just in case. She took long steps as she entered the airport, both to stretch her legs and to make a beeline for the nearest ladies' room.

Marco was only a few steps behind her, tugging his own bags along. His long legs allowed him to easily keep pace with her.

She glanced back, and saw that his attention was on the screen of his smartphone. They'd just come across the first restroom, so rather than lecture him about the dangers of texting and walking, she said, "I'll be right back. Can you keep an eye on my bags?"

"Sure." He barely looked up from his screen, but leaned against the outer wall near the restrooms.

Shaking her head, she ducked into the ladies' room.

Once she'd taken care of her needs, she washed up and took a look at her reflection in the long mirror over the sinks. Her face held evidence of the exhaustion she bore from the long flight. She didn't know which had been worse, being up in the air so long or having Marco be so quiet the entire time. He'd barely said three words to her during the flight. She knew he must be stressed out about the security breach, but she couldn't understand why he'd been treating her so coldly. After everything they'd shared, his outward attitude stung.

When she returned to where she'd left him, he was still there scrolling through his phone.

Joi was about to inquire about Chloe's whereabouts, but before she could form the sentence, the young assistant came running up, gripping her oversize hot-pink duffel.

"Sheesh, I should have done what y'all did and just brought a carry-on," Chloe gushed. "The crowd around the baggage carousel is outrageous."

Joi smiled. "I'm glad you're here. I thought I was going to have to go looking for you. How was your flight?"

Chloe grinned. "This was my first international flight, and my first time in business class. So no complaints."

"Good to hear." Joi turned her attention to Marco. "When and where are we supposed to meet the driver that's picking us up?" He'd told her that Royal was supplying a chauffeured car to get them from the airport to bank headquarters in the city.

Marco didn't respond, still busy tapping away on his smartphone screen.

Joi tapped him on the shoulder, resisting the urge to jab him a bit harder than was necessary.

After a few pokes, he looked up. His eyes were vacant as he said, "What?"

She rolled her eyes. "I asked you when and where we're supposed to meet the driver."

He pointed. "Right outside that door, in about ten minutes."

"How long a drive is it?"

He shrugged. "A little over two hours." Then he returned his attention to his phone.

She knew from her conversation with him the day before that they could have changed planes here to fly into Limón, but they'd both agreed that the less time they spent in the airport, the better. He'd brought her into his office to discuss his boss's request that they report to bank headquarters, and despite the seriousness of the situation, he'd at least shown her a hint of a smile. She closed her eyes, remembering the way he'd eased her close to him, buried his hands in her hair and kissed her until she'd felt weak in the knees.

Watching him now, she noted how much his mood seemed to have soured since then. *How long is he going to keep doing this?* She had no interest in contemplating whatever funk he was in any longer, because she and Chloe were there to do a job. So she turned away from him, focusing her attention on the glass door, searching for any sign of their driver.

After a few moments of scanning, she saw a man in a dark uniform and driving cap enter the door, holding a sign bearing the name Alvarez. She jabbed Marco to get his attention, then started moving toward the driver, pulling along her small wheeled suitcase. As soon as they got loaded into the black SUV parked in the pickup lane, they climbed into the vehicle. Chloe took the passenger seat, while Marco and Joi settled into the backseat.

A sliver of black leather separated their thighs, and even though they weren't touching, it was easy for Joi to feel the heat rolling off his body. He glanced her way briefly, wearing the same frown she'd seen when they'd left Charlotte, then turned to look out of his window. With a sigh and a shake of her head, Joi did the same.

The vibrating of her phone against her hip drew her attention away from the passing scenery of San Jose. Pulling the phone from her pocket, she saw her mother's number flashing on the screen. "Hello?"

"Joi? Where are you, baby?"

She smiled. At least now she wouldn't have to endure a silent ride all the way to Limón. "Hey, Mama. I'm in San Jose, and we're on the way to Limón."

"Sounds like you're riding in a car."

"We are. It will take us a couple of hours but it's less hassle than having to change planes and go through another airport."

"You were supposed to call me as soon as you touched down, Miss Lady."

She chuckled, deciding not to tell her mother that Marco's foul mood had distracted her from keeping that promise. "Sorry about that. If it's any consolation, I've been on the ground for less than an hour."

Emma Green Lewis was known for many things; taking excuses wasn't one of them. "I'll let you slide this time, if you bring me back something nice. You know I've never been to Costa Rica."

"I'll bring you something back, don't worry."

"All right. Your daddy says hi, and bring him something, too."

Joi laughed. "I will. Love you, Mama. I'll check in with you in a day or two."

"Love you, too, baby. Oh, and Joi?"

"Yes, ma'am?"

"Your sister told me about what's going on between you and the man you work for."

Tension crackled through Joi's body, making her go stiff in the seat. Leave it to Joanne to go blabbing her business to their mother, as if the situation wasn't complicated enough. Placing her fingertips to her temple, she sighed. "Oh, did she?"

"Yes, she did, and watch your tone, Miss Lady."

"Sorry." She fought to keep the annoyance out of her voice. Without turning her head, she let her eyes dart to her right briefly, toward Marco. Having her mother lecture her about their relationship while he sat right next to her made her feel as awkward as a sinner in church.

"All I'm saying is, be careful. Don't let your emotions overrule your good judgment, baby."

"I understand, Mama."

"Good. I'll talk to you soon."

Disconnecting the call and tucking her phone away, Joi didn't dare turn Marco's way. She could feel the heat burning her cheeks, and she knew they must be beet red. Emma Lewis loved her daughters fiercely, and protected them accordingly. Little did she know that Joi had already crossed the boundary with Marco, and that they were now lovers. No matter how she tried, Joi couldn't shake the feelings of attraction she held for him. She'd thought making love with him would cleanse her of her urges, but now she'd discovered the hard way that giving in to her desire had only served to intensify it.

In the front seat, Chloe chatted amicably with the driver, but the backseat remained as quiet as a tomb. Settling into her seat, she went back to regarding the passing scenery. The sky was crystal blue and cloudless, and the warm sun shone down over the lush green land. It was beautiful, and she vowed to take some time to sightsee once the security breach was rectified.

And as the vehicle rolled on, she tried her best to ignore the handsome, cologne-scented, but stubborn man sharing the seat with her.

From his seat behind Chloe in the truck, Marco spent the entire ride to Limón looking at the screen of his phone. He had dual reasons for doing so. He was searching through stories of banks taken down by serious security breaches, and trying to figure out how to keep his branch from becoming the subject of such a story. He sensed that Joi was probably put off by his stoic manner, but he would have to deal with that later. Right now, his main concern was preventing the downfall of his bank, and his career in finance.

When they arrived in town, the driver first took them to their hotel to check in. Once they'd done that, and deposited their bags in their respective rooms, they returned to the car for the short ride to bank headquarters. During the drive, Marco felt a smile spread across his face in spite of his worries. Seeing the old familiar sights of the city he called home comforted him like a balm.

Soon the building housing Royal Bank and Trust's international headquarters came into view. The seven-story steel-and-glass structure was octagonal in shape, making it stand out against the other more traditional buildings situated around it. The driver pulled into the lot, driving up to the roundabout in front of the building and parking at the curb. As the driver opened their doors to let them out of the vehicle, Marco passed him a twenty-dollar bill as a tip.

As Marco, Chloe and Joi approached the building, he held open the glass-and-metal door and gestured for his traveling companions to go in ahead of him. "After you, ladies."

Joi gave him a look that held a mixture of annoyance and confusion, but went inside as he'd instructed.

Seeing her expression made him realize he'd likely have a great deal of explaining to do later. But for now, he entered the building and led the way to the elevator bank.

Their steps echoed on the stone floors as they moved farther into the interior of Royal's headquarters. The high ceilings were accented with steel cross-beams, as well as several spherical modern art pieces, suspended at intervals and held up by thin steel cables of varying lengths. The walls were painted a muted shade of gray. Instead of hanging paintings on the wall, square-shaped chunks of quartz and granite had been set into it, forming a straight border halfway between the ceiling and the floor. He'd always loved the unique design of the building, which had been created and executed by a premier local architectural firm.

"Wow. This place is amazing." The comment came from Chloe, who was busy taking in the sights as they walked. "Never seen anything like it."

Marco waved at the desk clerk as they passed through the reception area. "Trust me, it's very reflective of the personality of the chief executive." Sal was a visionary, and he ran his bank in a way that few other financial executives would ever dare to attempt. Most of his board members and branch presidents were his close personal friends, and he never tried to bully, railroad or otherwise disrespect them.

He reached out to tap the call button for one of the three elevator cars, then stepped back. After a few moments, the center car arrived, and again, he waved the ladies ahead of him. As the two women moved past him to enter the elevator, he let his eyes drop to Joi's backside, clad in a professional but close-fitting black pencil skirt. The way the fabric skimmed over her curves made him recall the silken feel of her hips filling his hands as he made love to her. Her body was built for pleasure, and he wanted no other man to experience her splendor. As the blood rushed to fill his manhood, he recognized the mistake of letting his eyes linger there. Drawing his gaze up, he entered the car with them and pressed number seven on the keypad.

They stepped out on the seventh floor and into the corridor that led to Sal's penthouse office suite. In the vestibule waiting area of the space, Marco stopped briefly to chat with Elena, Sal's administrative assistant. After he'd introduced Elena to Joi and Chloe, Elena escorted the three of them to Sal's private office, then left.

As they entered, Sal stood from the humongous

leather throne behind the equally gigantic mahogany desk. "Marco. Good to see you, man."

Marco moved over to shake hands with his friend and boss. "Hey, Sal. Sorry it had to be under these circumstances."

Sal gave a dismissive shake of his head. "I have the utmost faith in the team. We'll straighten it out. Besides, the other branches haven't been affected, so this is apparently an isolated incident."

A smile touched Marco's lips. This was what he loved most about working for Sal: his optimism. Any other bank executive in this predicament would likely be having a nervous breakdown, but Sal somehow managed to keep things in proper perspective.

Sal slapped Marco on the back before strolling past him to greet the ladies. "You must be Ms. Lewis. Salvatore Perez, at your service." Sal stuck his hand out.

Joi offered him a small smile. "Yes, I'm Joi Lewis, owner of Citadel Security. I'm happy to meet you." She gestured to the young woman standing next to her. "This is my tech assistant, Chloe Ramsey."

His brow knitting with confusion, Sal shook Chloe's hand. "The pleasure is mine, but I thought your name was Karen Russell."

Joi's eyes widened, and she glared at Marco.

Suddenly every pair of eyes in the room landed on Marco's sheepish face.

Knowing the time to come clean had arrived, Marco spoke up. "Sorry, Sal, I should have clarified. Ms. Russell couldn't travel because she's recovering from a fall. Miss Ramsey is her second in command."

Sal turned back toward the ladies. "Well, whatever

the case, welcome to Limón. Join me, won't you?" He gestured to the small sitting area centering the office.

The sitting area consisted of a brown leather love seat and two matching armchairs, all situated around a stout mahogany coffee table.

As the four of them took up seats. Marco sat with Sal on the love seat, and Joi and Chloe each occupied one of the chairs. Both women pulled out something to take notes. The technically inclined young assistant took out her phone and a stylus, while Joi produced a small legal pad and pen from her purse. Marco watched as Joi slung one long black hose-encased leg over the other, presumably to form a solid base of support for the legal pad. Whatever her motivation, the action enticed Marco, tightening his groin so much that he pressed his own legs together.

Elena appeared again, carrying a tray containing four glasses of ice water, complete with lemon wedges. After setting the tray down on the short-legged table, the assistant disappeared from the room.

For the next hour, Marco participated in a candid discussion about their options for remedying the security breach. The entire time, he stole glances at Joi's slender legs, and at the way she pursed her glossy lips when she was thinking about something.

Suddenly, she looked up from the legal pad, and her gaze met his. Her brown eyes sparkled with amusement, and he realized she'd caught him staring. Straightening in his chair, he turned to Sal. "When are we going to start the process of searching the server for the source of the problem?"

Sal glanced at his gold wristwatch. "It's late, almost six. The tech team will start leaving for the night pretty soon, so I suppose we'll tackle the heavy work tomorrow."

Joi raised her hand. "Mr. Perez, if I may."

"Yes?"

"Citadel is dedicated to providing the best service for our client. Our motto is 'Always on Guard,' and we strive to live up to that. So if any members on your team are willing to stay, my technologist and I are willing to start work tonight."

Marco's brow hitched. They'd been traveling all day, and he knew she must be hungry and tired, yet here she was offering to work late.

Sal looked similarly surprised. "Ms. Lewis, are you certain? I'm sure you've had a long day."

She tucked her legal pad away. "Yes, Mr. Perez, I have, and yes, I'm certain. I want to make sure Royal gets the very best service, and as owner, that starts with me."

His expression betraying the good impression Joi had made on him, Sal nodded. "All right, Ms. Lewis. I must say I'm impressed by your dedication."

Marco had to agree.

"Thank you, sir." Joi stood, smoothing out her skirt. "Just show me to the place I'll be working."

Sal chuckled. "Not so fast. I insist that you all take an hour for dinner first. Then feel free to begin."

She nodded. "Fair enough."

Now Chloe was on her feet, as well. "Please tell me there's a cafeteria in this building."

Marco got up from his seat. "There is. Follow me and I'll show you the way."

As they left Sal's office, Marco watched Joi walk the corridor in front of him. She hadn't been in the building for very long, but already her strides communicated her confidence in her ability to handle the job she'd been assigned.

He smiled, knowing his valiant lady was in her element.

And when she finally set aside work, he'd show her just how much he appreciated her unique capabilities.

Chapter 14

When ten o'clock rolled around that night, Joi was still slumped over one of Royal's laptop computers, with Chloe and one of Royal's IT guys looking over her shoulder. She reached up to stifle a yawn, then used the back of her hand to swipe at her bleary eyes. "Take over, Chloe. I think I've been staring at this screen entirely too long."

"Got it."

As Joi moved out of the way, the young assistant slid smoothly onto the stool she'd been occupying.

Standing for the first time in the past ninety minutes, Joi extended her arms over her head, hoping to stretch the kinks and tension out of her shoulders. She'd tossed aside her blazer a while ago, and rolled up the sleeves of her lemon-yellow button-down. Her discarded pumps were on the carpeted floor beneath the desk where Chloe now sat, typing away on the laptop's keyboard.

She glanced across the large room, and saw that Marco was still present, as well. He looked pretty disheveled, but she supposed that was to be expected at this time of night. He'd taken off his sport coat and tie, and loosened the top three buttons of the crisp white shirt he wore. His attention was currently focused on the screen of another computer, and as she watched him, he raked one large hand through the dark riches of his hair. *Mmm. I kind of like this unkempt look.* Her lips curved up into a smile. It only took a few more seconds of staring at him before she remembered why he looked so appealing. If memory served her, he'd looked similarly unkempt after their passionate night of lovemaking. That thought sent a tremor through her body, tightening her nipples. She took a few deep breaths, thankful for the modesty inserts she always wore in her bra when she was working. It had only taken one business meeting in a chilly conference room to teach her that valuable lesson.

Watching Marco work, head down and a look of determination etched on his handsome face, Joi couldn't help staring at him. She knew she should get back to the task at hand, but right now, all her energies were being employed just to keep her from drooling. *How can a man be so fine and so maddening all at once?*

"Ms. Lewis. Ms. Lewis?"

Joi snapped out of her trance at the sound of Chloe's voice. Jerking her head around to face the young assistant, she blinked a couple of times to clear her bleary eyes. "I'm sorry, what did you say?"

Chloe grinned. "The night shift starting to get to you, boss lady?"

She nodded. That explanation was serviceable for the moment. "My apologies. I wasn't paying attention. Now tell me what you were saying again."

"I was saying that it looks like a worm attacked Ms. Russell's program, and that's what took down the firewall protecting the branch systems."

Joi could feel her face scrunch in confusion. "A worm? But Karen's program is unique. She designed that thing from the bottom up. How did someone even know to send a worm to attack that specific program?" Now the gears of her mind were turning again. She'd reached out to Karen a couple of times over the last few days, but Karen's medicine had her sleeping almost around the clock.

The flaxen-haired Royal technologist working with them shook his head. In a voice thick with the local Spanish accent, the man commented, "This seems very suspicious. Almost like…"

Joi stood, completing his sentence. "Sabotage."

By now, Chloe's eyes had gone completely round. She swiveled around on the stool she was sitting on. "Holy crap."

"Holy crap is right." Joi rested her chin in her hand for a moment, feeling the synapses firing inside her brain. "We've got some digging to do." She pulled out her phone. It was late back home, but at this point she had no choice but to call Karen, and pray she was awake.

The phone rang a couple of times before Gabe answered. "Hey, Joi. You're in luck. Karen's just waking up."

A smile spread over her face. "Great, Gabe. Put her on, please."

A few moments later, Karen's voice came on the line. "Hello? Gabe says you and Chloe are in Costa Rica?"

"Yes, yes. I'll explain that in a minute. First, how are you feeling?"

"Still sore, and in and out of sleep, but I'm okay. Man, only I would take a fall and end up being out of work when I could have gotten a free international trip." Based on Karen's tone, she was genuinely disappointed to have missed it.

Joi knew that there was little time for banter, so she moved on. "Karen, the reason Chloe and I are here is because your security firewall for the bank was taken down by a worm yesterday morning. Shut down the ATMs and all the teller computer terminals in the building."

A small shriek came from Karen's end of the line. "What? How in the world did this happen? My program is custom-built and impervious to this kind of stuff."

"Unfortunately it's not quite as impervious as we thought. Chloe and I are with Royal's tech team right now, and we need you to tell us what we have to do to straighten this out. After all, Virtual Lockdown is your baby."

Karen sighed. "I can't believe a worm came after my baby. It will be easier for me to explain to Chloe, so put her on the phone."

Joi passed the phone to Chloe. "It's Karen. Take notes."

Chloe nodded as she accepted the phone, pulling

out her own smartphone and a stylus. Balancing Joi's phone in the crook of her shoulder, she listened to Karen's instructions and transcribed them onto her device using the stylus. Joi looked on, amazed at the seemingly natural technical inclinations of the younger generation.

Once Chloe disconnected the call with Karen, she returned Joi's phone. "Basically, we're going to have to access Karen's cloud, get the backup copy of the software and make a modification to it. The hardware folks will have to come in and replace the hard drives on the teller terminals and the ATMs at the branch, and then we can reinstall the improved software."

Joi nodded, thinking of how the cost of all those new machines would likely not be a point in her favor. She could only hope Citadel wouldn't be kicked to the curb over it. "What about the worm?"

"We can delete the malicious program, but Karen says that the only way it could have been compromised in the first place is from within."

Joi's brow hitched. "You mean someone who works in the branch?"

Chloe nodded. "She was about to tell me what staff members had direct access, but then I heard snoring on the line. Her husband says her medicine put her back to sleep."

"That means we'll have to wait until tomorrow to get the names." Joi scratched her chin. "Anyway, do what you can to take down the worm for now, and we'll deal with the rest later."

"Got it." Chloe and the Royal technologist turned their focus back to the laptop they were working on.

By now, it was just after eleven thirty. Joi, noticing

how dry her mouth felt, was about to take a sip from her plastic water bottle when she saw Marco walking in her direction. He'd buttoned his shirt, and his sport coat was slung over his forearm. The closer he came to her, the more she felt an entirely different type of thirst rising within her.

When he reached her, he asked, "How are things going? Any new discoveries?"

Joi recounted what she and Chloe had just learned from their long evening of strip-searching the software files, and their conversation with Karen. While she spoke, Marco listened with intent.

"Sounds like you're done for the night." Marco fixed her with a direct gaze as he spoke.

She was already stepping back into her shoes and slipping into her blazer. While a low-level buzz of energy hummed through her body, she was beyond ready to leave the confines of the bank headquarters.

"Do you want to ride with me back to the hotel, so we can get some rest?"

She shrugged. "I know I probably should, but I'm too wired to sleep."

Marco placed his large open palm on her forearm. "At least walk out with me. You can decide on the way."

She felt a smile touch the corners of her mouth. Gathering her purse and the case holding her clipboard and other supplies, she tapped Chloe on the shoulder. "Will you be able to get back to the hotel?"

The blond technologist working with her offered, "We'll have a car bring her as soon as she's done, and I'll personally escort her."

"Thank you." Joi glanced around at the remaining

staff. There were four women and two men, including Chloe's partner, still at work. Knowing that Chloe was in good hands, Joi followed Marco out of the room and into the corridor, toward the elevator bank.

In the silent hallway, he turned to her as they waited for an elevator car. "Are you sure you're not tired?"

She chuckled, wondering where this line of questioning was going. "I feel like I've gotten my second wind."

He reached out and clasped both of her hands in his. As the elevator doors chimed and slid open, he spoke. "Then walk on the beach with me, Joi."

She let her fingertips graze the stubbled line of his jaw. "That sounds lovely."

Marco called the car service, and had the driver deliver him and Joi back to the hotel. The Hotel De Sol's prime beachfront location on the shores of Limón made it his preferred accommodations whenever he visited home. As a full-grown single man, he found staying at his parents' house to be awkward at best and unbearable at worst.

When they exited the car and started for the hotel's lobby, he stayed a few steps behind her so he could watch her walk. The delicate, sensual sway of her hips held his attention, fueling the fires of passion already burning inside him. She was a lot of woman, and he was just the man to fill her needs.

She stopped at the elevator bank and jabbed the up button.

He strolled up next to her. "Meet you back down here in fifteen minutes."

She gifted him with a soft smile and nodded. When

the doors opened, she stepped inside the car. "Aren't you coming?"

Their rooms were both on the tenth floor, but with the way he felt, Marco knew better than to isolate himself in an elevator car with her. "I'll take the next car. If I get in there with you, you may never want to come out."

"I'm sure I would get off, though." She winked.

His groin tightened instantly at the naughty little double entendre.

The doors began to close, but he got a look at her sly smile before they shut fully.

By the time he got his own elevator car up to his room, he was so hard he had to think of basketball statistics so he could walk straight.

He took a few minutes to strip off the clothes he'd been wearing and slipped into a pair of casual black slacks and a white linen shirt. With a pair of sandals on his feet, he returned to the lobby to meet Joi.

He saw her standing by the lobby's rear door, wearing a long, flowing floral-print sundress. Whisper-thin straps bisected her shoulders, baring her collarbone and arms.

She turned his way as he approached, and reached out her hand for his. The simple gesture touched him deep within. He felt a smile spreading over his face as he took her hand and led her through the hotel's building and across the grounds to the beach.

Soon they were under the light of the full moon, walking along the strip of soft white sand bordering the Caribbean Sea. The moonbeams lit the water's surface, illuminating the frothy white waves as they rose and fell. The sound of the water's movement soothed his mind, and he relished hearing it up close again.

He turned his head, watching her stroll along beside him. The breeze coming off the water played through her hair, lifting the dark waves of it so that it swirled around her head like a halo.

"It's beautiful out here." She made the remark while looking reverently out over the water's dark surface.

He gave voice to his own thoughts. "Almost as beautiful as you." He saw her expression change, and even in the dim light, he knew she was blushing. "I remember coming here as a boy with my parents. We came here at least two weekends every month, to picnic and enjoy ourselves."

"Do you have any brothers or sisters?"

He shook his head. "I'm the only child of Cruze and Iveliss Alvarez."

She looked up at him then, seeming concerned. "Didn't you ever feel lonely?"

"Far from it. My parents adored me, and I enjoyed every bit of attention they gave me. They played with me, and I always had friends from school. But at home, whatever I had was my own, and I liked that."

Joi chuckled. "Actually, that explains a lot about your personality. Apparently all that attention from your parents has turned you into the charmer you are today."

"I like to think so." He brushed away a lock of hair the wind had blown into her face. "What about you? I believe you said you had a sister."

"I have an older sister, Joanne. It was just the two of us growing up. Poor Daddy was the only male in the house, and I'm sure we drove him bonkers."

That statement intrigued him. "What makes you say that?" They were still walking, keeping a good distance from the water's edge.

"We were so different. Joanne is a girl in every traditional sense—tall, graceful, feminine. But me, I was a tomboy who climbed trees, didn't like dresses and got into fights."

He stopped walking, turning to face her. "Do tell."

She looked a bit embarrassed, but said, "Let's just say I don't take kindly to people calling my sister names. So when Jerry Brown called her a giraffe, I knocked him out."

"How old were you then?"

She shrugged. "Ten or eleven. He was fourteen, and hasn't shown his face in town since."

He didn't know which was funnier, the tale she told, or the poker face she wore while telling it. Laughter boiled up inside him, tumbling out of his mouth. Soon they were both laughing at her story.

When they finally stopped laughing, she raised her free hand to her mouth, stifling a yawn. "Oh, boy. I think my second wind has petered out."

He glanced at his wristwatch. "It's almost three in the morning. I've kept you up long enough. Let's get you inside and into bed."

She didn't protest, and they walked back up to the main building of the hotel.

This time they shared an elevator car, and spent the entire time locked in a heated embrace. He sprinkled his kisses over her forehead, her eyelids and her cheeks. Then he tilted her head up so he could kiss her mouth, tasting the sweetness there. When the doors slid open on the tenth floor, they reluctantly broke the kiss.

His arm draped around her shoulders, he escorted her to the door of her room. They'd been assigned rooms at opposite ends of the corridor, so he knew he'd have a bit of a walk to get to his own room, but he wanted to prolong their time together.

In front of the door, she turned to face him. A glimmer of desire danced in her dark eyes. She lifted her arms, put them around his neck. "Do you want to come inside?"

He sucked in a breath, thinking her sassy mouth would be the death of him. She had no idea just how much, and in how many ways, he wanted to *come inside*. "That's the best offer I've had all day, but we've got to be back at Royal in a few hours."

She stuck out her bottom lip in a mock pout.

"We both know that if I come in, we're not going to sleep. Get some rest, Dulce." He ran the tip of his index finger along her jawline, reveling in the sweetness of her presence while he still could.

"You're awfully honorable, Marco Alvarez." Her expression had softened into one of understanding.

He pecked her on the forehead. As she unlocked her door, he shooed her inside. "I hope you'll remember that, and reward me accordingly when the time comes."

She giggled as she let the door swing shut.

He turned, drew a deep breath and took the long walk to his own room.

Chapter 15

Wednesday morning, Joi was back in the same room in Royal's headquarters, working with Chloe and the tech team as they attempted to disarm and dismantle the malicious worm that had eaten its way through Karen's cybersecurity program. They'd managed to shore up the bank's central defenses, disallowing the worm from penetrating the firewalls of the other branches. That meant the breach wouldn't go any further, and that was an excellent start.

Joi found doing this during the day shift a bit easier, due to the bright sunlight streaming in through the wall of windows that made up the western side of the room. She'd purposefully set up her makeshift workstation so that she'd be angled toward the light, and with a few sips from the steaming cup of coffee next to her, she finally felt fully awake.

Marco was behind her, out of her line of sight on the other side of the room, but she still sensed his presence as if he were in her personal space. Her body still hummed from the remembered sensations of his touch and his kiss. He'd been right to go back to his room in the wee hours of the morning, because they both needed sleep so they could focus on their work. Still, she'd been so aroused last night that she'd lain awake for quite some time before sleep claimed her. She knew that working so hard on four hours of sleep would eventually catch up with her, but right now, she had a job to do.

All around her, laptops were open, as were notebooks. The sounds of clicking keys and the murmur of several conversations provided the background noise to her own work. Being in this environment reminded her of how much she enjoyed being in control of the physical aspects of security. *This tech stuff bores me to tears. Thank God for Karen.*

Thinking of her business partner reminded her to give her a call. Chloe was very capable, and she and the Royal technologists had made a lot of headway in disabling the worm, but no one knew the software like its creator. Grabbing her phone from the table, she picked it up to dial Karen.

Before she could swipe the screen, the phone rang, and Karen's number appeared. Joi answered right away. "Hello? Is that you, Gabe?"

The answer was prefaced by Karen's chuckle. "No, it's me this time. I was awake enough to make the call on my own."

Joi heaved a sigh of relief. "Oh, thank God. We

need you to help us out so we can get this damn worm taken care of."

"Of course you need me. Ultimate Lockdown is my brainchild. I can see Chloe's already accessed my secured cloud to get the backup copy. Who's making the modifications?"

Joi shrugged. "I guess Chloe's doing it, but you know the technical stuff is not in my wheelhouse."

"I'll talk to her in a minute. Anyway, I need to let you know about the staff that trained on the software when I came in to set it up."

Joi straightened in the metal folding chair she was sitting in. "Yes, we need that information, because this is looking more and more like an inside job."

Karen's tone changed to one of disgust. "I trained the three senior staffers at the branch on the software. They watched me install it and everything. Those three were Roosevelt, Nancy and Donetta. And I think I know just where to lay the blame."

Joi's ears perked when she heard Donetta's name. Donetta Charles, the bank's loan officer, rarely ever spoke to any of the other staffers. And beyond that, she hardly ever came out of her office, or even opened the door. It seemed that the bank staff was accustomed to Donetta's antisocial ways, but as a security manager, Joi had been aware of Donetta's odd behavior from the first time she'd met her.

"Joi, are you still there? You got quiet on me."

"I'm just thinking about what you said. I've always been a little leery of Ms. Charles. I think my next call is going to be to Yolanda. She may have found something in the security footage that can help."

"Sounds good." Karen yawned. "I'll call Chloe's

phone. That way I can work with her and your line will be freed up. Later, girl."

"Bye, hon. Feel better soon." Joi ended that call and immediately began another one with Yolanda. By the time she pocketed her phone, she had a satisfied smile on her face. While combing through ten days' worth of security footage, Yolanda had found just the footage they were looking for.

She rose from her chair, intent on going to Marco with the news. As she crossed the room, her thunder was stolen by Chloe, who jumped up from her seat in front of one of Royal's company laptops and squealed.

"We've got it, y'all! We eviscerated that worm!"

Chuckling at both her youthful exuberance and her use of the word *eviscerate*, Joi joined in the applause and cheering that took over the room. After this ordeal, she was pretty certain Karen would hire Chloe on a permanent basis once she graduated from Johnson C. Smith with her masters degree.

When the excitement started to die down, Joi stopped off to congratulate Chloe briefly, then made her way to where Marco stood speaking to another Royal staffer. As she approached, the other man drifted away, leaving the two of them alone.

Directing his full attention toward her, he spoke. "You look like you have something to say."

Staring into his handsome face and mesmerizing gaze, she almost forgot what she'd come to tell him. After a few long seconds, her brain kicked into gear again. "I spoke to Yolanda, and she found something very interesting in the security footage."

He folded his arms over his chest, his dark brow furrowed. "Really. And what was that?"

"Donetta Charles, your loan officer, brought two flash drives into the bank. We think those drives delivered the worm to your computer systems."

His jaw hardened, as if he felt betrayed. "Flash drives. Have they been recovered?"

She shook her head. "No. The footage shows her removing them after the fact. We assume she discarded them, but she won't be able to deny the footage."

"And your guard could get all this from the security footage? Flash drives are pretty compact, and hard to see on camera."

"My guards are the best in the business, and they are very thorough. I know she combed every inch of the frame, and with digital imaging, it's easier to blow up a particular frame of the image for closer inspection."

"Then I'll put in a call to the authorities."

"Yolanda already did. I imagine there will be a warrant out for Donetta's arrest before we get back to the States."

His expression softened. "Once again, you and your staff have impressed me. Citadel is quite an outfit."

That made her smile, but she couldn't resist teasing him. "Really? So does this mean you're admitting you were wrong to judge me and my company based on the past?"

He rolled his eyes, yet he acquiesced. "Yes, I admit I was wrong. Initially I doubted you, based on my very limited knowledge of who you were. But you've shown yourself to be as professional and as capable as the job demands."

She propped her fists on her hips, raised her chin

with a hint of defiance. "Apology accepted, Mr. Alvarez."

He chuckled, shaking his head. "You are too much."

Heat crackled between them. She wanted to grab him by the arm and run away to some dark, secluded corner of the building where they could kiss and paw at each other like two hormone-crazed teenagers.

Sal strode into the room, and that thought fled as he made a beeline straight for where she stood with Marco. Sal's bright smile made her think someone had informed him of their victory over the worm.

"Ms. Lewis, I hear your staff has destroyed the malicious software."

She returned his smiled. "Yes, we have, sir. Just a few moments ago."

Sal stuck out his hand. "Impressive work, Ms. Lewis. You and your staff are to be commended."

"Thank you, sir." She matched his hearty handshake. "Your satisfaction as our client is the best gift we could receive."

The older man's salt-and-pepper brow furrowed. "Nonsense. The best gift that you and your staff could receive is the permanent security contract for all three US branches of Royal Bank and Trust."

Her heart somersaulted in her chest. "Excuse me? I must have misheard you, Mr. Perez."

"Let me be clearer, then. I want Citadel Security to handle the contracts for my branches in Charlotte, Los Angeles and New York." He nudged her gently with his elbow. "Did you get it that time?"

She fought back the happy tears rising in her throat. "Yes, sir, I did. Thank you. Thank you so much." Securing a contract this lucrative would mean a very secure future for Citadel and her staff, and that was all she'd ever wanted for her business. Remembering the size of her staff, and of her offices, she spoke. "We'll be glad to take on the contracts, as long as you don't mind giving us a bit of time to restructure. I want to make sure we're equipped to meet Royal's needs."

"Can you be ready to take over in four months?"

It was a stretch, but she knew that if they buckled down, she and her staff could get it done. Knowing she'd be a fool to say otherwise, she accepted his terms. "Yes, sir. That won't be a problem."

"Excellent." He turned to Marco. "Set her up with whatever she needs. I'll have accounts payable forward an initial payment to her."

"Got it, Sal." Marco slapped his boss on the back as the older man walked away. Turning back to her, he said, "This is cause for celebration."

She knew just the sort of celebration she'd like, but since they weren't alone, she asked demurely, "What do you have in mind?"

"Dinner, maybe a bit of dancing…" His eyes met hers. "And afterward, whatever you like."

She felt her tongue dart out to wet her lips. "Sounds appetizing." And it did.

The longer she looked into his eyes, and felt the masculine heat rolling off his body to touch hers, the more she knew that getting through the rest of the workday would not be an easy task.

As evening waned into the night, Marco looked around the table at the faces of his colleagues and friends. Several of Royal's technologists, along with Joi and Chloe, had joined him for a dinner to celebrate their hard-won victory over the malicious software worm.

He turned his head slightly to the right, watching Joi interact with the other people sitting around the table. She wore a bright smile as she spoke, her words tinged with humor. All eyes were on her. It seemed as if everyone at the table had fallen under her spell. He couldn't really blame them, because he too was mesmerized by her every gesture. He watched the flex of her glossy lips, wondering how much longer it would be before he could taste them again. While the restaurant offered a large selection of decadent desserts, only Joi could satisfy his sweet tooth.

He craved the taste of her mouth, of her skin. He craved the feel of her body pressed against his own. The longer the meal continued, the higher his desire rose, and he didn't know how much longer he could stand it.

His tongue darted out, sweeping over his lower lip just as Joi glanced his way. Her sensual smile at the gesture made him fling up a plea to the heavens that the gathering would end soon.

Marco's prayers were answered when one of the technologists yawned and mentioned being tired. Others joined in, and before long, the group had gotten their separate checks and began to break up. He took a few moments to phone their car service to transport him, Joi and Chloe back to their hotel. With their bills settled and the summoned car idling at the curb in front of the restaurant, the three of them left.

Mindful of the young woman riding with them, he

managed to keep his hands to himself for the duration of the ride. When the car deposited them in front of the hotel, they entered the main building and crossed the lobby to the elevator bank. All three of their rooms were on the tenth floor, and he spent the entire ride up there pondering how they might avoid an awkward situation. Glancing at Joi, he surmised she might be thinking the same thing, based on her thoughtful expression.

On the tenth floor, Chloe solved the problem for them. Stifling a yawn, she announced, "I'm beat. See you guys in the morning."

"Remember, Mr. Perez gave us, and the entire tech staff, the day off as a reward." The reminder came from Joi.

Delight sparkled in Chloe's hazel eyes. "Fantastic, because I think I'll sleep until Friday." With that announcement, she trudged off to her room. She'd been assigned a room two doors down from the elevator bank, so they heard the clicking sounds of her door closing and locking just a few moments later.

He turned his gaze to Joi, feeling a smile tug the corners of his mouth. "Well, that was convenient."

"Wasn't it?" She draped her arms around his neck, and for the first time in exactly twenty-one hours, she pressed her lips against his. They had only two more days in this coastal paradise, and she didn't want to waste time.

He kept the kiss brief, knowing that if he didn't, he might raise her little black pencil skirt right there in the hotel corridor. "Your room, or mine?"

Her lashes fluttered. "Neither. I really want to go back out on the beach again."

A glance at his watch showed that it was well past one in the morning. "What is with you and hanging out on the beach in the middle of the night?"

She sensed the teasing in his tone, and gave him an equally playful punch in the forearm. "Whatever. Just change your clothes and take me down there."

"You got it." He turned around, and the two of them went to their separate rooms to get out of their work clothes. He threw on a clean pair of black slacks and a classic white tee. Moments later, they both returned to the corridor.

When he saw her standing there in the plum-colored strapless dress, he stopped. The fabric wasn't clingy, but it wasn't loose, either. The dress fell to ankle length, baring the curve of her shoulders and the length of her arms to his eyes. The garment was simple, but it did much to accentuate the beauty of the woman wearing it.

He moved near her, and held out his hand. She took it, a demure smile lighting her beautiful face. If she could read his thoughts, she'd know that he wanted nothing more than to strip the dress away and bare her body to his touch.

They rode the elevator back downstairs, taking the same path they'd taken previously, until they found themselves back on the beach. Again, they kept their hands locked together as they strode along the band of white sand. Tonight, a hazy half-moon hung above them to light the way.

Looking at her in the dim light, he felt his heart pounding in his chest. There was something about her that made him feel like a schoolboy, nothing more than a bundle of hormones.

She caught him staring at her. With humor dancing in her big brown eyes, she asked innocently, "What is it?"

He shook his head. "Nothing. Just wondering what makes you tick."

A soft chuckle came in response. "Remember the story I told you about socking that little boy who called my sister a giraffe?"

He did. "Of course. I also remember witnessing your takedown skills firsthand."

She rolled her eyes at him and laughed. "Anyway, that's how I've always been. I guess you could classify me as a tomboy, especially when you compare me to my sister. Joanne has always been all manners and delicate sensibilities."

He noticed the edge in her voice as she spoke about her sister, and it made him want to understand her better. "And what are you?"

She shrugged. "The short, rowdy one with a mean left hook. I'm pretty much the opposite of my sister. She's super feminine, but I just don't see myself that way."

Looking down at her, he could feel the confusion knit his brow. "What do you mean by that?"

She snorted. "Come on, Marco. When's the last time you heard a woman praised for her ability to put a man twice her size in a submission hold? Or to break his pelvic bone with a well-placed knee?"

His brow hitched. "You can do all that?"

"Yes, and if you don't stop teasing me you're going to find out firsthand."

He straightened up right away. "All kidding aside,

Joi, I don't think femininity and physical prowess are mutually exclusive."

She turned away from him, and it looked as if she were watching the waves roll in. Over the roar of the churning waters, he barely heard her soft reply. "You're the only man I've heard say that."

He shrugged. "Maybe other men are stupid. Or maybe they're just terrified of your ability to over-power them."

They rounded a bend in the shoreline, and moved diagonally up a rise to a secluded area of the beach. There was no one out there, at least not within his line of sight. But even if there were other people out at this time of night, the dunes situated around the little hilly spot would keep them from being seen.

She stopped walking, and so did he. Looking up into his eyes, she asked, "And how are you different from those other men, Marco?"

He released her hand, let his open palms slide up her arms to her shoulder. Feeling the tremor that ran through her at his touch, he spoke. "What makes me different is that I know a real woman when I see one. And you, Joi Lewis, are undeniably, one hundred per-cent, fully feminine."

Her soft smile melted his heart. "Well. Aren't you the charmer?"

"Just speaking the truth, Dulce." He smoothed his right hand upward, until it rested on her cheek.

Her hand moved to cover his as she moved closer to him, draping her free arm around his waist. The heat of her nearness penetrated the fabric separating them, and he could feel his groin tighten reflexively.

Her eyes glittering, she tilted her face and met his

gaze. "Kiss me, Marco." The words escaped her lips on a breathy sigh.

"With pleasure," he murmured, and an instant later, he crushed her lips with his own.

Chapter 16

Joi could feel Marco's hand cupping her cheek, and the strong arm pinning her body flush to his, as the kiss deepened. Her rising desire had emboldened her to ask for his kiss, and now, he was delivering big-time. Her lips parted, allowing his tongue to enter her mouth and stroke against her own. The sensations elicited a low, crooning moan from her.

He eased away, still holding her close. The dark pools of his eyes were focused solely on her, as if they were the only two people in the whole world. He moved back a few inches, releasing his hold on her as he took a seat on the sand near her feet. With his long legs bent and his ankles crossed, he patted his lap, gesturing for her to sit.

She obliged him, easing into the nest of his lap and facing the right side. He pulled her close, draping her legs over the crook of his arm, as his other arm supported her upper back. Her bottom made contact with the apex of his powerful thighs, and she released a small gasp when she felt the familiar hardness pressing against the sensitive flesh of her hip.

"I'm ready for you, Dulce." He breathed the words into her ear. "But first, I want to play…to make sure you are ready for me. Is that all right?"

She nodded as a sensual shiver ran down her spine. If his mission was to make her arousal rise, he was already off to a brilliant start. Already, she could feel the goose bumps breaking out on the surface of her skin at the mere anticipation of his skillful touch.

He moved to let her legs drop, freeing one hand. With the tall dunes of sand sheltering them from prying eyes, she watched as he eased the top of her dress down, revealing the thin, sheer fabric of her strapless bra.

"Dulce, you're beautiful." He murmured the words softly as his fingertips mapped the curve of her breasts, just above the sheer fabric. He drew her closer, letting his kisses retrace the path of his fingers. Her eyes closed, and she arched as the pleasure shot through her like an electric current.

He adjusted her in his lap until she had a solid base of support, then reached around her to unclasp the bra. He paused momentarily, sought her consent again. "Can I…"

"Yes…" She didn't wait for him to finish his question because, God, she wanted this. When he unclasped the bra and tossed it aside, baring her sensitive flesh to the breeze flowing over the surface of the water, she groaned. Then she dissolved into soft cries as his warm mouth settled over one of her nipples.

He lavished the breast with attention, his large hand cupping it as he savored her nipple. When she thought she'd die from the pleasure of it, he stopped, but only long enough to turn the same treatment on her other breast. By the time he drew away, she lay half-dressed and panting in his arms.

She opened her eyes, found him watching her.

The wicked smile and the flames dancing in his eyes relayed his enjoyment at the sight of her, arching and breathless in the moonlight. "Dulce, you are a vision."

His flattery only served to send more heated blood to her already swollen core. She was so mindless, she couldn't formulate a coherent reply.

"Let's see what more I can do to make you moan." Now one large hand scuttled up her leg, to the hem of her dress. She knew exactly what he was doing, and she offered no resistance as he gently raised the hem, baring her trembling thighs to the night air. Each inch of skin he touched was seared, branded as his.

She swallowed, felt him hook his thumbs beneath the waistband of her panties. He tugged them down and removed them. With hooded eyes, she watched him fold them neatly and tuck them into the pocket of his slacks.

First the gentle breeze touched her core, then, his even gentler fingertips. At the first touch, she shivered, not from being cold, but from being oh so hot. His fingers meandered and played, circling and teasing the bundle of nerves centering her womanhood. Her legs fell apart, widening to give him unobstructed access, and the pace of her breathing increased. Over the sounds of her own throaty sighs, she heard him uttering soft, sensual endearments in Spanish, which only increased her passion.

The tide of ecstasy rose within her, lapping at the shore of completion. *Yes,* her mind screamed. Yes to everything he was doing, and everything he had planned for her this night. A thousand times yes.

As if sensing her impending crisis, he leaned down to whisper in her ear. "Let go, Dulce. Come for me."

At the sound of his voice, her control faltered and her body shook with the force of a release that radiated out from her core to the very tips of her fingers and toes. She called his name on a strangled cry, writhing and twisting as his strong arms supported her weight.

When she came back to awareness, she saw him watching her in the muted light. The color of the sky above heralded the coming dawn, and she wondered just how much time had passed. The only sounds she heard were the crashing of the waves, and their own heightened breathing.

Finally, he spoke, with a hint of humor in his voice. "I think we should go inside now."

She stretched, sat up in his lap. "Did I fall asleep?"

He nodded. "For a bit. You looked so peaceful I didn't want to disturb you. Ready to go in?"

She adjusted her dress to cover her exposed breasts, then stood, tugging the hem of her dress down. When she'd effectively concealed her nudity, she reached down and picked up her discarded bra from the sand.

He got up as well, still fully dressed. Her eyes zeroed in on the prominent bulge below his waist, and a tingle raced through her core.

Catching the direction of her gaze, he smiled. "The sooner we get inside, the sooner you can have it."

She returned his smile, swept her open palm over the bulge. "Then let's go to my room."

Joining hands, they made their way back inside the hotel and up to the tenth floor. Inside the confines of the elevator car, they kissed and stroked one another, keeping their bodies as close together as their clothing would allow. The elevator doors opened on the tenth floor, and they maneuvered down the hall toward her room, kissing and fumbling like love-struck newlyweds the entire way. It took some effort, but she finally tapped the electronic key against the lock and opened the door. They both backed into the room, falling onto the bed in a tangle of limbs as the door slammed shut behind them. She kicked off the thong sandals she'd been wearing, not sure of where they landed, and not caring.

She was beneath him, barely aware of his weight as he kissed her senseless. When he released her and raised up on his hands, she immediately reached up to drag his white shirt up and over his head. Her palms burned as she toured them over the hard, muscled lines of his chest. To pay him back for the sensual torture he'd dealt her earlier, she used her thumbs and forefingers to tease his nipples.

He sucked in a breath. "You are truly wicked, Dulce."

"Why don't you teach me a lesson, then?" She lay back on the surface of the bed, awaiting whatever method of instruction he deemed appropriate.

In response to her sassy decree, he snatched her dress away. Leaving her nude form reclining on the bed, he stood to quickly remove his sandals, and to strip out of his pants and underwear. From his pocket, he produced a condom, which he rolled on to protect them. When he rejoined her on the bed, she purred with anticipation. No man had ever filled her with such a complete feeling of safety, of feminine vulnerability, of molten-hot desire. Marco was everything she never thought she needed, and she wanted everything he had to give, forever.

Forever.

She winced as the thought passed through her mind. This was no time to be thinking about attachments, not now that she had so much to do to prepare her business for national expansion. But despite what logic told her was right, her heart knew otherwise. She'd fallen in love with Marco, and there was nothing she could do to change it.

Marco centered himself between Joi's shapely thighs, bracing his body weight on his elbows to avoid crushing her. She looked so gorgeous, laid out beneath him like a veritable buffet of pleasure. His body begged for her, urging him to plunge inside her warmth, but he refused to be rough with her. Despite her views on who she was, and her defensive abilities, she was still his Dulce, his delicate blossom.

He leaned down, placed soft kisses over her brow, her closed eyelids and the bridge of her nose. Despite the insistence of his throbbing manhood, he held back, taking her on a slow ride toward ecstasy.

The air held the citrusy scent of her perfume, and the intoxicating scent of her arousal. He grazed his fingertips over her body, down the center of her chest, then lower, drifting over her stomach until he reached her core. There, he eased his index finger into paradise, feeling the silken heat of her desire. Her hips rose from the bed as he gently moved the finger in, then out.

"Do you like this, Dulce? Do you want more?"

"Yes..." she whimpered. "More..."

So he obliged her, enjoying the way she reacted to his touch, and the knowledge that her core was so wet and primed for his entrance.

She hummed low in her throat. Placing a hand on either side of him, she pressed down, tilting his pelvis closer to hers. The tip of his manhood brushed against her core, and he growled.

"Now, Marco." The urgency in her tone spoke of her desire.

Obliging her, he flexed his hips, entered her in a single slow stroke. Each of them gasped as their bodies joined, and he pressed forward until he'd reached maximum depth. Sheathed within the tight confines of her body, he felt as if he'd come home after a long absence. He rocked his hips in an easy, deliberate rhythm, reveling in the sounds of her sharp gasps.

He loved making love to her this way, loved the way she sang for him on the wings of pleasure, loved the way her body felt sheltering his. He loved the way she spoke, the way she moved and the way her lips pursed when she was deep in thought.

I love everything about her.

I love her.

He continued to move, stroking her with all the passion he felt, even as he pushed away those thoughts. Love meant commitment. Commitment meant settling down. Settling down meant responsibilities, sacrifice and so much more.

No. He wouldn't think about that now, not while the red-hot pleasure rose inside him, threatening to make him erupt like Vesuvius at any moment. He turned his focus back where it belonged, on making love to the beautiful woman lying beneath him, and giving her all the pleasure she could stand.

She trembled, and her eyes went wide before rolling back in her head. He knew she was on the brink of another orgasm, so he rotated his hips, increasing the depth and speed of his strokes. He wanted her to shatter, wanted to watch the glow of pleasure spread over her face.

Suddenly she arched. "God, Marco!" Her body stiffened, then a tremor ran through it, and he felt her inner muscles gripping his shaft.

The waves of pleasure hit him then, and he rode them to his own release, his body pressed against hers. His shouts mingled with her moans, until the wonder passed and the room fell into silence again.

A little later, he extracted himself from her body, and moved so they could get into a more comfortable position in the bed. The sun had fully risen by now, and the rays of light penetrated the sheer curtains covering the sliding door that led out to the balcony.

Joi had fallen asleep beneath him, and her soft snores barely broke the silence. As he eased beside her and draped his arm over her form, he was taken aback by the sight of her.

Lying nude in the hazy sunlight, she looked like a goddess. Her bronzed skin glistened with a light sheen of perspiration, and while he looked on, mesmerized, she shifted a bit.

Her eyelids twitched, then she opened her eyes. Sleepily, she asked, "Why are you staring at me?"

Not knowing what else to say, he told her the truth. "Because you're so beautiful, I can't look away."

With a catlike stretch, she offered him a smile. "Flattery will get you everywhere, Marco."

He tugged at the covers, adjusting things until they could both slip beneath them. When their bodies were cocooned beneath the patterned comforter and white sheets, he lay on his back and drew her into his arms. Her head rested on his chest, and he played his fingertips through the riotous mass of her hair. A feeling of peace and contentment settled over him as he held her close to his heart, and he got a sense that this was where she belonged.

He didn't know how or when it had happened, but he'd let himself fall in love with her. He knew it with every fiber of his being, and he was surer of it than he'd ever been of anything in his life.

Up until she'd shown up at his office to put in her proposal for the security contract, he'd thought he would spend the rest of his life playing the field. Commitment had never been part of his plans for the future, because he hadn't wanted to be saddled with the "burden" of being responsible for a wife, let alone children. Now, he'd begun to rethink his entire way of life. Would being a husband, and dare he think it, a father, really be as stifling and confining as he had assumed? Or could the love of a wife and family open the door to his heart, and to a level of happiness he'd never thought possible before?

Somehow, this petite powerhouse, mouthy, tough and wonderful, had come into his life and turned everything upside down. He'd thought he'd known who she was when she stepped into his office that day, but he could not have been more wrong. Only this time, he was actually glad to have been mistaken, and even happier that she'd stayed around long enough to show him how stupid he'd been to misjudge her.

He opened his mouth, set to tell her that she'd stolen his heart, and that he couldn't live without her. But before he could form the words, he heard her snores rising again. She'd gone back to sleep, and after what they'd shared, he didn't want to deny her the rest.

So he snuggled down into the soft feather pillow, and held her close, his body sheltering her as she slept.

Chapter 17

Joi yawned and opened her eyes, squinting against the bright sunlight. Unraveling the cocoon of blankets around her, she rolled from her side to her back. Her freedom of movement revealed the empty spot in the bed next to her. She sat up, rubbed her eyes and looked around the room. Marco was nowhere in sight but the closed bathroom door made her think he must be in there.

Sure enough, the sounds of running water emitted from behind the door. She reached up with both hands, attempting to tame her wild hair before he made an appearance.

The bathroom door swung open, and Marco stepped out with the white hotel towel wrapped around his waist. Her eyes traveled over the hard, muscled lines of his chest and arms appreciatively. She could easily recall the feel of his body against hers, and as he strode toward where she sat on the bed, the hairs on the back of her neck stood on end.

Self-satisfied smile on his face, he said, "Good morning, sleepyhead."

"Good morning, yourself." She drew the crisp white sheets up around her body to fend off the chill in the room. "What time is it?"

"It's about one thirty." He sat on the edge of the bed, leaned over to give her a soft kiss on the cheek. "Good thing we had the day off today."

She didn't bother to tell him that his lovemaking had caused her exhaustion. Based on his expression, he already knew. Not only did he know, but he seemed quite pleased with himself. Looking at him now, she knew things had changed between them. Last night they'd both been swept up in the waves of passion, but in the clear light of day, the truth of her feelings for him was bound to surface. She had no indication he shared her feelings, but she knew she would only be able to hold them back for so long.

Her stomach growled loudly, so she set aside her complex emotions for the moment. She leaned to her right, stretching her arm until she could reach the room service menu on the nightstand. "I don't know about you, but I'm hungry."

He chuckled. "After what we did last night, it's understandable. And yes, I could eat, too." He eased closer to her, draping his arms casually around her waist.

Choosing what to eat proved difficult, not because there were so many choices, but because he insisted on nuzzling her neck. The prickly sensation of his chin, moving against the crook of her shoulder, was enough to ruin her concentration.

He must have sensed a struggle, because he gave her a bit of space, but left his arm around her. Finally able to make a decision, she reached for the phone. "Do you want anything?"

He scratched his chin. "Just get me the grand breakfast."

Her eyes widened when she realized he'd ordered the largest meal possible, but as far as she and her body were concerned he'd earned it. Removing the handset from the cradle, she dialed the extension for room service and placed their order. When she hung up, she found him watching her with heated eyes.

She pursed her lips. "Marco, room service will be here within half an hour."

He drew her closer to him, a wicked smile spreading across his face. "More than enough time to make you moan, Dulce."

She wanted to protest, but could only sigh as he drew down the sheet and took one of her nipples into his mouth. With skill, he proved his words true. By the time room service knocked on the door, he had indeed made her moan.

Since she was still recovering from her orgasm, he answered the door. A few moments later, he wheeled a small cart into the center of the road. The cart was laden with trays and plates filled with their breakfast offerings. Getting her bearings again, she stood and retreated to the bathroom to take care of her own needs. In a few moments, she'd washed up and slipped into a pair of sweatpants and a T-shirt.

He flipped on the TV, and they ate their breakfast in convivial silence. Her plate of fluffy scrambled eggs, wheat toast and turkey sausage sated her appetite. Watching Marco chow down on a towering stack of pancakes, along with sausage, eggs and fruit, she wondered where on his trim frame he stored that much food.

After they ate and returned their dishes to the cart, she slid open the door leading to the small balcony. Stepping out, she drew a deep breath of the fresh air, which held the scent of the water. She placed both hands on the railing and enjoyed the feel of the breeze lifting her hair. With her eyes closed, she let the sunlight warm her face.

She sensed his approach moments later. His arms slid around her waist as his chest came into contact with her back. He remained bare from the waist up, but the towel he'd been wearing was gone, replaced by his trousers. She leaned into him and let his steady strength support her. In her day-to-day life, she was seen as tough, hard and capable. But in his arms, she felt soft, feminine and vulnerable. He had a certain quality that made her feel balanced and safe.

"My Dulce..." He muttered the endearment into the crown of her hair.

Her heart pounded in her chest like a mallet striking a timpani. More than anything, she wanted to tell him how she felt. She needed him to know that she loved him.

She turned in the circle of his arms, prepared to bare her soul to him.

The look in his eyes stopped her, made her snatch back the words before she had a chance to say them.

She knew that look. Ever since she'd started dating as a teen, she'd seen men wear that look.

Its meaning was clear. *Guilt.*

She drew a deep breath, inhaling the moist air and the masculine scent that always clung to him. "God, Marco. What is it?"

He hesitated, as if struggling to choose his words. When he finally did speak, he was brief, but the words held an almost crushing weight. "Forgive me."

Fear mixed with curiosity rose within her. Hesitantly, she asked, "Forgive you for what?"

He dropped his gaze, let his arms fall away from their position on her hips. "I judged you so harshly for walking away from Ernesto."

A small amount of relief began to bloom within her, but the bloom was immediately clipped by his next statement.

"In reality, you were right to walk away, and I knew all along. I should have been praising you for following your instincts, not calling you disloyal."

Her brows came together, anger and confusion warring for supremacy inside her. "Marco, stop speaking in riddles. Say what you mean."

A low, rumbling sound came from his throat. Then he swung his gaze back up to meet hers. "Ernesto wasn't in love with you. He needed to marry someone in order to get his hands on his inheritance."

"What!" She prayed she'd misheard him.

"He told me about it several weeks before he proposed. Look, I didn't know you back then, and I needed…"

"You son of a bitch!" she shouted at him, then pressed her palms against his chest to put distance between them. As he stumbled back, she stormed past him, reentering her hotel room. She strode immediately to the room's small closet and dragged out her suitcase.

He was on her heels, but he wisely remained a few feet away from her. "Joi, please. If you'd just let me explain…"

She scoffed, a sound meant to communicate her utter disgust with him. "Explain what? How you've been holding a grudge against me all these years for trusting my own heart? How you almost caused me to miss out on the biggest opportunity I could get for my company?" As she spoke, she busied herself tossing her things into the suitcase, because she couldn't wait to get back to Charlotte.

He dropped his hands to his side, his expression grim. "So, you're just going to leave? Just like that?"

Unshed tears began to sting her eyes. She leveled him with a hard gaze. "My work is done here. There's no reason for me to stay. I'll be in touch with Mr. Perez early next week. As for you—" she pointed to the door "—get dressed, get your crap and get the hell out."

"I'm so sorry, Dulce."

How dare he call me that now? The pet name that had seemed so endearing only hours ago now seemed to burn her ears. "Whatever." To emphasize how done she was with him, she grabbed his shirt from among the twisted bedclothes, bundled it up and threw it at him. All she wanted was for him to leave, right now, before she started blubbering.

He caught the shirt in midair, then sighed, as if resigned to his fate. He said nothing more as he dragged the shirt on and gathered his shoes, wallet and smartphone. With a last glance in her direction, he opened the door and left.

The moment the door slammed shut, tears began to course down her face. In a way, she was relieved that he'd revealed his true, conniving nature before she'd had a chance to say those three words. Unfortunately for her heart, not saying them aloud didn't change anything. She still loved him, and now she knew they could never be together.

She began packing, moving around the room to gather her strewn items of clothing while the tears blurred her vision. Because if she had her way, she'd be on the very next available flight back to Charlotte.

And when she got home, she'd start the process of restructuring her business, including setting things up so that she'd never have to see Marco Alvarez again.

Marco stood in the door of his parents' bedroom, waiting for them to finish getting ready. As he leaned his shoulder against the door frame, careful not to snag the jacket of his black tuxedo, he sighed. The Herreras' celebratory gala was due to start in less than an hour, and with traffic being what it was, they needed to get on the road soon. At this pace, they were going to be unfashionably late.

He could feel the frown settling over his face, where it had been for the past day and a half since Joi had thrown him out of her hotel room. He missed her fiercely, but considering the fact that he'd been wrong, and that she'd probably toss him off the balcony, he hadn't attempted to go back again. How could he approach her now and ask her forgiveness, when in reality they both knew he didn't deserve it?

If he hadn't already promised Ernesto that he'd attend tonight's party, he would have shut himself into his own hotel room with a cigar and flask. That would mean ruining two relationships in as many days, so there would be no getting out of his promise. So for now, he braced himself to suffer through what was sure to be a long evening.

His mother, Iveliss, sat at her vanity, fussing over the shimmering length of her gray hair. Dressed in a beautiful and tasteful cream-colored ball gown, she looked amazing and much younger than her sixty-four years. Apparently she intended for every single stray hair, regardless of length, to be contained in the tight bun at her nape.

Cruze, his father, was fully dressed in his tux with his salt-and-pepper hair neatly combed. Still, the old man was pacing the room in only one shoe, searching for his left wingtip.

On any other occasion, watching his parents putter about the house while preparing to go out would tickle him, and he'd probably be laughing at this point. The carefree amusement eluded him this time, though. He knew Joi would probably never speak to him again, and because of that he felt empty and humorless.

His eyes scanning the floor of the room, Marco spotted his father's missing shoe. The tip of it peeked out from beneath the satin bed skirt on their king-size bed. Meandering over to the spot, Marco picked up the shoe and handed it to his father. "Looking for this?"

Cruze smiled. "There it is. Thank you, son." He sat down on the edge of the bed, tossed the shoe down and slid his black-sock-covered left foot into it. "Well, I'm ready."

Marco jerked his head in his mother's direction. "Mom isn't."

Cruze stood then, walking over to where his wife sat. He placed his hands gently on her shoulders. "Ivy, you are a vision of loveliness. Don't do another thing, my love."

Her cheeks visibly reddened, accompanied by a coy smile. "Cruze, you charmer." Setting aside her silver-plated hairbrush, she let her husband help her to her feet. Then she stepped into his embrace, placing a soft kiss against his cheek.

Marco's expression softened as he viewed his parents' interaction. Both of them were well into their sixties, but their love for each other was blatant and strong. As a younger man, when he'd looked at them together, all he'd seen were the sacrifices they'd made for each other, and to give him a better life. As he'd grown older, though, Marco had observed another side of marriage: the sheer joy of loving someone, and being loved in return. The moment became bittersweet as he wondered if that kind of happiness would ever be his.

"The car's been waiting outside for a little while, so we can go when you're ready." While Marco didn't begrudge his parents their love, he couldn't take much more of it for the moment. Especially since he knew he'd be playing the role of third wheel tonight.

The three of them left the bedroom, with Cruze and Iveliss holding hands and walking ahead of Marco. They descended the staircase, and Marco moved around his parents to hold the front door open for them. The balmy night air, thick with the perfume of Iveliss's prized orchids, greeted them.

Outside at the curb, a black sedan idled, awaiting

their approach. The driver, who stood leaning against the trunk, opened the doors for the Alvarez family, and once they were all inside, he got the drive under way.

The sedan was equipped with two bench seats in the rear, which faced each other. Marco sat across from his parents, looking out the back windshield as the vehicle rolled through the streets of Limón.

As the car stopped at a traffic signal, Cruze turned his attention on his son. "When are you going to tell us what happened with your young lady?"

Iveliss seemed to share her husband's curiosity, because she silently regarded her son.

Marco groaned, but kept his tone in check out of respect for his parents. "I'm not. Suffice it to say I ruined things with her, and she'll probably never speak to me again."

His father's expression showed his displeasure. "Marco, if you love her, then you know what you have to do."

"Dad, if you don't mind, I'd prefer not to speak about this right now." He knew that if the conversation continued down this path, the path where his father lectured him about going after Joi and winning her back, a shouting match wouldn't be far behind.

Cruze's brow furrowed, but he threw up a hand in surrender. "Fine. But, son, do fix your face. Just because you're miserable doesn't mean we want to look at that scowl all night."

Marco took a deep breath, and put on his best fake smile. "Better, Dad?"

"Actually, yes." Cruze turned his attention back to his wife.

The rest of the ride passed in silence. After the

driver let them out of the sedan, in front of the ritzy Tortuga Lodge Hotel, Marco straightened his bow tie and prepared to keep the false smile plastered on his face all evening long.

The atmosphere inside the ballroom was as festive as the milestone demanded. A large gold banner hung along the north wall, reading Herrera Incorporated: Celebrating 40 Years. Three long tables had been set up, displaying a sumptuous buffet, overflowing with savory dishes and a bevy of sugar-laden desserts. The buffet was staffed by white-coated chefs, dispensing the gastronomic delights in proper portions.

The tables around the room were dressed in gold and black, and waiters wearing black suits and gold ties floated amongst the guests, seeing to their every need. Yes, the Herreras knew how to throw a party, and tonight was no exception.

Following his parents, Marco strode around the perimeter of the ballroom, until he came to the table where the Herreras were holding court like a king and his queen. While the Herreras and the Alvarezes exchanged pleasantries, Marco went straight to Ernesto, who sat at his mother's side looking as bored as a rambunctious child forced to listen to a long sermon.

"Marco. I'm glad you could make it, man." Ernesto stood, shaking hands with his friend. "This party was seriously lacking in the hot women department, but I know you brought some with you." He looked around expectantly.

Shaking his head, Marco scoffed. "I don't travel with a harem, you know. And tonight I don't even have a date."

Ernesto's brow rose by at least two inches. "What

do you mean, you don't have a date? Marco the Magnificent, coming to the party of the century solo? I don't believe this."

"Believe it." He had no desire to elaborate, because this night was already going to be difficult enough without going into the gory details.

Ernesto chuckled. "I'm just teasing you, man. Actually, I have a little surprise for you. There's someone I want you to meet."

Curious and confused, Marco followed Ernesto to a table a few feet away. Seated at the table were three young women, and when Ernesto placed his hands possessively on the shoulder of one of them, Marco's eyes widened.

A smiling Ernesto announced, "Marco, meet my wife, Anita. Anita, my love, this is my dear friend Marco."

The dark-haired, green-eyed Anita stood, offering her hand to him. "I'm pleased to meet you, Marco."

"Likewise." Marco pushed his shock aside long enough to kiss her offered hand. Then he turned to Ernesto, with questioning eyes.

Ernesto helped Anita back into her seat, then placed a soft kiss on her brow.

Marco waited only a few seconds before grabbing the end of Ernesto's tuxedo jacket and tugging it. "Sidebar, sir."

They moved away from the table of women, and as soon as they were out of earshot, Marco asked, "When did you get married? And is it the real thing this time?"

With a chuckle, Ernesto slapped him on the back. "I thought about telling you on the phone, but seeing your face has made keeping the secret well worth it!"

Marco gritted his teeth. "Ernesto, answer me."

"I've been married for three months, and yes, it's real. Anita is the love of my life, and I'm so glad she agreed to marry me."

Marco looked at his friend, and immediately recognized the truth of his words—he was actually in love. Taken aback, he shook his head in wonder. "What can I say? Congratulations, my friend."

"Thank you. And, get this, my parents love her, too. So everything's wonderful." Ernesto's eyes were still on his wife as he spoke.

"I wish I could say the same." Marco drew a deep breath. While he was happy for Ernesto, it was hard for him to accept things as they'd turned out.

Ernesto's gaze landed on his friend's face, and sympathy penetrated his expression. "Sorry to hear that, man. Is there anything I can do?"

And just like that, the lightbulb illuminated inside Marco's head. Tossing his arm around the shoulders of his old friend, he smiled. "Actually, there is."

Taking a breath, he began to explain the situation with Joi.

Chapter 18

With a pen in one hand and a stack of papers in the other, Joi turned sideways on the sofa and stretched her legs out in front of her. The venetian blinds at her living room window were open, allowing the afternoon sunlight to stream in. It was another chilly late-autumn Saturday, where it looked much warmer outside than it actually was. But the temperatures had risen a bit since the previous week's cold snap, finally making it back into the mid-fifties typical for the area this time of year.

It was warm enough that she could have gone out, but she didn't want to. Since she and Chloe had returned from Costa Rica two days ago, she hadn't had much desire to do much of anything. She hadn't even gone into her office yesterday, nor had she swung by any of her job sites to check in with her guards. All of the catching up she'd done had taken place by phone, allowing her the space she needed to accept the new state of things.

She'd fallen into bed Friday afternoon, when the exhaustion from the travel and two all-nighters she'd pulled in Limón finally caught up with her. Wrapped in her own blankets and the comfort of her own bed, she'd slept for fourteen solid hours. Now, rested and fed, she planned on starting the process of expanding Citadel to accommodate the scope of the new contract she'd earned from Royal.

She'd called Karen from the airport in San Jose, before boarding her return flight, to let her know about their new contract. Karen, who was off the pain medication and would soon return to work, had been overjoyed at the news. Hearing about Chloe's contribution to their victory over the malicious software, Karen had insisted on offering the assistant a permanent position as soon as it could be arranged. Joi was in wholehearted agreement with that, since Chloe had shown herself to be an important asset to Citadel's cybersecurity department.

Joi settled into the microfiber cushion, with a small wooden lap desk resting on her thighs. She set the papers down, and started to jot notes about all the tasks she'd need to take care of for the expansion. In the margin of the page, she began to sketch out a rough timeline that would allow everything to be taken care of in the four-month period Mr. Perez had suggested. As she wrote, she reminded herself that this was just a draft, and that she'd go back later to add in more detail.

An image of Marco's face floated into her mind, breaking her concentration. Despite her best efforts, she could not push the image, or the memories of what they'd shared, away. The remembered sensations of his touch, his kiss and his hardness filling her so completely were potent, and not easily dismissed. Sighing aloud, she tucked her pen into the base of her haphazard ponytail. *So much for getting any work done.* Frustrated, she let her head drop back on the armrest behind her.

The sound of someone knocking on her door drew her attention before she could settle into studying her ceiling. Setting the lap desk aside, she climbed to her feet and went to answer the door. A glance through the peephole revealed Joanne standing on the front porch, tapping her foot. Knowing her sister was not going to go away, she unlocked the door and swung it open. "Joanne, what are you doing here? Saturdays are your busiest day at the shop."

Entering the house, Joanne shrugged out of her coat and hung it from one of the row of hooks mounted next to the door. "I know, but my manager is handling the shop today. My baby sister just returned from an international trip and I want to hear all about it!" She gave Joi a peck on the cheek before moving farther into the house.

Joi followed her sister, who'd made a beeline through the living room, straight to the kitchen. Watching her rifle through the fridge, she folded her arms over her chest. "Really, Joanne? Don't you have food at your house?"

Turning to her with a bottle of pinot noir in one hand and a bag of cheese cubes in the other, Joanne replied, with a straight face, "Girl, no! Don't you remember? I live in a house with a grown man and a little boy going through a growth spurt. I'm lucky they haven't eaten my countertops."

A giggle bubbled up and escaped Joi's mouth, despite her less-than-sunny mood. Her sister could always be counted on to say something crazy, but she knew the statement was tinged with honesty.

Joanne, having dumped the cheese onto a platter, was now searching the cabinets. "Where are you hiding the crackers? Because I know you have some in the house."

Shaking her head, Joi helped her sister pile the tray with crackers and mixed nuts, then fetched wineglasses for the two of them. Soon she was back on the couch, moving her work out of the way so her sister could join her.

Holding her filled glass, Joanne said around a mouthful of cheese and crackers, "So, tell me about your trip. I've never been to Costa Rica."

She shrugged, taking a sip from her own glass. "Really, I worked most of the time I was there. The only things I saw were the airport in San Jose, the bank headquarters and my hotel." *And the strip of beach along the Caribbean Sea, where Marco made me scream his name...*

Ever perceptive, Joanne cocked a brow. "There's something you're not telling me, little sister. Spill the beans."

Joi turned away, choosing to stuff a handful of salted nuts into her mouth.

Joanne stared at her for a few moments, squinting her eyes. Then her hand flew up, index finger extended. "Aha! Something happened between you and Marco, didn't it?"

Joi groaned.

"Didn't it?" Joanne repeated herself, her tone revealing that she had no plans to back down from this line of questioning.

Aware that she'd been backed into the proverbial corner, Joi sighed. In as few words as possible, she explained to her sister what had occurred: the night of passion she and Marco had shared, and the revelation of his betrayal, along with her subsequent early departure from the paradise that was Puerto Limón.

When Joi finished Joanne's eyes were still locked on her, but her expression had softened considerably.

Joi groused, "Go ahead and hit me with the 'I told you so.' Might as well get it out of your system."

Instead of lecturing her, Joanne set her wineglass aside and opened her arms. "Come here. You look like you could use a little love, sis."

Joi put down her wineglass and leaned over into her sister's embrace. Before she knew it, the bitter tears started to fall. "I love him, Joanne. I really do, but I can never be with him now that I know what kind of person he really is."

Patting her back, Joanne offered her sister comfort. "I'm sorry things turned out this way, Joi. Usually I like being right, but this one time I think I would have rather been wrong. I hate to see you hurting."

And she was hurting. It hurt to know that Marco had been so dishonest, and it hurt to know she'd never feel his touch on her skin, or his kiss against her lips again. But what hurt more than anything was the unspoken love for him that she still held within her. It was true, it was intense, and try as she might, she just couldn't seem to make it go away.

"What do I do now, Joanne?" She moaned the words through her tears.

"I don't know, sis. But I'm here for you." Joanne tightened her embrace, rocking from side to side.

And as the tears continued to stream down her face, Joi wondered if she could ever go back to life the way it used to be, before Marco entered her world and yanked it loose from its moorings.

As Marco navigated the maze known as the parking lot of Charlotte Douglas International Airport, he tried to keep his focus on driving. It was Sunday afternoon, and his return flight from San Jose had landed about an hour prior. Due to the glut of incoming flights landing as the weekend faded into the workweek, the loops of roadway that funneled vehicles away from the terminals and back onto the highway were clogged with traffic.

When he'd left last week to go to Royal headquarters, he hadn't expected to return with any extra baggage, other than maybe a few souvenirs. Circumstances had dictated otherwise, because now he had a passenger riding in his car with him, and it was not the one he'd expected.

Ernesto, busy scrolling through something on the screen of his phone, didn't bother to look up as he spoke. "Whatever happened with your loan officer?"

He shook his head as he thought of the duplicitous Donetta Charles. "After the guards turned the security footage over to the police, they arrested her. She's in the county lockup for now."

Ernesto chuckled. "No flash drive is going to get her out of this jam."

Marco had to agree, but it was still the weekend, and he didn't want to talk about work now. The only thing on his mind now was Joi, and how he could get her to hear him out. That was the reason he'd insisted Ernesto accompany him back to Charlotte.

"So are you sure this is going to work?"

He shook his head, aware that Ernesto was asking about his plan to get back in Joi's good graces. "No, I'm not sure. All I know is that if I don't try, I'll never be able to get past this."

"Well, I hope I can help you make things right, man. I'm just sorry Anita couldn't come along." The new Mrs. Herrera had already planned a shopping excursion with her mother-in-law, the elder Mrs. Herrera.

Marco shrugged. "I understand. I didn't intend to interrupt her plans, or yours, for that matter."

"This is the first time I've traveled this far without her, since we got married. I already miss her." A smile spread over Ernesto's face as he looked up from his phone. "She's been texting me since we landed, and she misses me, too."

Marco shook his head, still trying to wrap his mind around the whole situation. The man sitting next to him was so different from the Ernesto he'd attended college with. The womanizing goof-off had now been replaced with a man of purpose. Ernesto obviously loved his wife, and would likely rearrange his entire life to gain her praise. He realized the change was a vast improvement, and inside, he had to admit he was a little jealous. What Ernesto had with Anita was just what he wanted with Joi.

Curious as to how the relationship that had changed

his friend's outlook on life began, Marco asked, "How did you meet Anita?"

Ernesto chuckled. "Actually, she came into the Herrera offices several months ago to apply for a position in the administrative office."

"Did you interview her?"

He shook his head. "No, my human resources manager did the interview, but I sit in on most of them. Anita was so overqualified that she didn't get the job, but I got her number that day and the rest is history."

The story made Marco smile. It seemed somewhat humorous to him that both he and his friend had fallen for a woman they met in the workplace. He supposed that in their lines of work, which led to them spending a great deal of time in the office, it made sense.

As he finally merged onto the highway, Marco had his first destination in mind. He and Ernesto had already grabbed something to eat before leaving the terminal, so there was nothing standing between him and making a very important purchase, other than the ribbon of road stretched out before him.

About half an hour later, he pulled into the parking lot of Josephine and Company, a high-end jeweler located in uptown Charlotte.

Ernesto tucked his phone away as Marco cut the engine, and looked up to see where they were. "I was shocked to hear the story of what went down between you and Joi, man."

"I know. Sorry I threw you such a curveball, but I wanted to be honest with you."

Ernesto waved him off. "I get it, man. And I appreciate your honesty. Like I said, I'm not mad. I never had strong feelings for Joi anyway."

"Still, I wanted to clear the air. I had to, if I'm going to have any chance at a life with her."

"You're serious about this, aren't you?"

Marco's eyes were on the sparkling gems displayed in the window of the store as he replied. "I've never been more serious about anything in my life." He fully understood the risk he'd be taking, but he prayed that between him and Ernesto, they could explain the situation well enough so that Joi would forgive him. Her forgiveness was his first goal, and if he could gain that, he felt hopeful that he could gain her heart, and her presence in his life, forever.

The two men climbed out of the car, and Marco used the remote to lock it before they entered the store.

Chapter 19

The conference room at Citadel Security was full for the first time in months as Joi and most of her staff sat around the long table. Her laptop open, she streamed an internet radio station that played hits from the eighties. She kept the volume low, letting the music provide some background noise for their conversation, because the upbeat music helped to calm her frazzled nerves. She couldn't help cracking a smile when The Bangles' hit "Manic Monday" began to play over the computer's speakers.

How appropriate.

Manic was a pretty accurate descriptor of her day so far. Not only was it the first day of the workweek, but it was Karen's first day back to work since her unfortunate fall had landed her in the hospital. Karen, with her wrist now encased in a flexible brace, was sitting next to Chloe, who was thrilled to have been given a permanent position due to her hard work on the Royal project.

Yolanda, Kim and Maxine, Joi's three most senior security guards, were also present at the table. Joi had asked them to be present because she knew she'd need their assistance in interviewing, vetting and hiring the new guards Citadel would need to meet the demands of the new national contract with Royal.

The six women seated around the table had spent the past two and a half hours going over the new contract. They had discussed strategies to expand Citadel's staff, and the possibility of opening a West Coast office in light of their new responsibilities at Royal's branch in Los Angeles. Joi's head was spinning, filled with so many ideas that she could barely type fast enough to keep up with them. In anticipation of that, she'd set up a small digital recorder in the center of the table, to record the conversation.

"Based on what we're taking on, I'll need to hire at least three more technologists." The comment came from Karen, who was leaned over her own open laptop. "That way I can have Chloe work here with me at the main office to handle most of our local accounts, and each branch of the bank would have a dedicated cybersecurity manager."

Joi nodded, typing that into the open document she'd been working on. "Sounds good to me. And if we can get one or two extra ones on an as-needed basis, we'll have some backup in case someone needs to take time off." She narrowed her eyes playfully at her friend and partner as she said the last two words.

Karen chuckled. "Don't worry. No more falls for

me. I hate hospitals and I've spent enough time there after this ordeal to last me the rest of my life."

Maxine interjected, "We're thinking the same thing as far as new guards go. If we want two per branch, and a few alternates, we'll need to hire about eight to ten."

"Agreed." Yolanda turned to Joi. "Are we still hiring only female guards?"

Joi smiled. "Yes, ma'am. That's what Citadel is all about, extending opportunities to women that they don't normally get, even though they're fully capable of handling the job. No matter how much we grow, I want to keep that core practice in place."

All three guards applauded, communicating their approval of her stance, and Joi executed a small bow from her seat at the head of the table. "All right, ladies. We need to get this stuff done. We're on a tight deadline. Four months isn't very long to pull off an expansion like this, but if anybody can do it, we can."

A few of them groaned, but everyone at the table did as she asked. Soon, the only sounds in the room were the clicking of computer keys and the subtle scratch of pens gliding over the surface of paper.

Joi got up from her chair, intent on getting a refill on her cup of coffee before she settled back into her own work. Mug in hand, she slipped out of the conference room and into the hall.

She'd just turned into the doorway of the break room when she heard the bell over the entrance chime, signaling that someone had come in. She did a quick spin, her gaze seeking out the visitor.

Her empty mug fell from her hand and crashed to the floor when she saw the two men standing in her lobby. One was a blast from her past, and the other could've been her future.

With the shards of broken mug scattered around her feet, she watched as Marco and Ernesto walked farther into the lobby. Ernesto hung back a bit, as if uncertain of how she'd react to seeing him, but Marco powered toward her.

Swinging her gaze from her ex-fiancé to the man who'd stolen her heart, she took in the sight of him. Marco was dressed in yet another expensive and well-tailored suit. The suit, the color of caramel, was only about three shades darker than his tan skin. He'd paired the suit with a crisp white shirt and a solid black tie. In his arms, he carried an epic bouquet of sterling roses that seemed to contain at least a hundred large blooms.

A few of the girls in the office had poked their heads out into the hallway, probably prompted by the sound of the mug shattering. Joi barely noticed them as she stepped over the bits of ceramic and tipped into the lobby to meet Marco.

When they came abreast of each other, he spoke. "Joi. I know you're busy, and if you don't want to talk to me, just say the word and I'll leave."

Just say the word? Easier said than done. Right now she couldn't remember how to talk, let alone formulate something to say. Seeing him standing there with that humongous bouquet and his heart on his sleeve had her feeling tongue-tied and vapid.

Taking her silence as permission, Marco set the flowers down on the coffee table in the waiting area, and gestured for Ernesto. As his friend approached, Marco spoke. "I thought the best way to explain what happened was to bring Ernesto here and get everything out in the open. Is that okay with you?"

She managed to bob her head up and down. Shifting her attention again to Ernesto, she finally found her voice. "Long time, no see."

Ernesto released an awkward chuckle. "Hi, Joi. It's good to see you again."

She didn't know if she agreed, so she didn't respond to that. She hadn't seen Ernesto since she'd made that famous fifty-yard dash, abandoning him at the altar. If he were hurt by her actions, he didn't show it. She'd always wondered how she would react to seeing him again, if the occasion ever arose. Now that it was happening, she found that her feelings for Ernesto were… neutral. She couldn't say she felt strongly about him, one way or the other. Marco, however, was a different story altogether.

As if wanting to fill the silence, Ernesto launched into a speech. "Marco asked me to come here and give you the whole story. What he said was true. I did propose to you to get at my inheritance, and I'm sorry. Now that I have someone in my life who I truly love, I realize how heinous my actions were. I hope you can forgive me." Having apparently said all he had to say, he took a large step backward.

Hearing the words from Ernesto somehow lightened the burden she'd been carrying since Marco had told her of the betrayal. "I appreciate that, Ernesto, and I forgive you." Releasing that small amount of bitterness into the universe felt pretty good, but she sensed there was more to the story.

Marco gently touched her shoulder. "What I didn't

tell you when we were in Limón is why I never alerted you to Ernesto's intentions back then."

She turned his way, clasped her hands in front of her and braced for what would have to be one hell of a good explanation.

"I needed money, badly. I was buried in student loans from getting my MBA, and Ernesto promised me that once the marriage took place and he got his inheritance, he'd pay off my student loans." Marco's gaze conveyed a degree of embarrassment as he made the admission.

The look in his eyes, and her own understanding of the struggle to pay for higher education, softened her heart right away. She lifted her hand, laid it alongside his jaw. "Why didn't you tell me that before?"

"I tried, but you were so angry by then, I couldn't get it out." His hand clasped hers, moved it so that he could place her open palm against his lips. "I paid Ernesto back the first year I worked at Royal."

She recalled the red-hot anger that had coursed through her that day, and the way she'd thrown him out of her room. It was true. She hadn't given him time to elaborate.

As his lips grazed her hand, she sighed at the familiar magic coursing through her body. "Oh, Marco."

"Forgive me, Dulce. Please." He made the entreaty in a tone as soft as his kisses.

She drew in a deep breath, taking a moment to consider his words. His remorse seemed genuine, and she did understand his actions, to a degree. She imagined it must have been hard on his male pride to admit that he'd once turned to a friend for financial assistance.

"I will never keep a secret from you again." A hopeful spark lit his dark eyes as he made the promise.

His declarations touched her, softening her anger and hurt. With damp eyes, she smiled. "All right. I forgive you. But you'd better stay in my good graces or I'm using you to practice my takedown moves."

He grinned at her teasing words. "Deal. But there's one more thing."

Her brow furrowed. "What's that?"

He reached into an inner pocket of his sport coat, and in a heartbeat, he'd fallen to one knee. The small black box he produced made her heart skip a beat. When he opened the box to reveal a glittering, heart-shaped solitaire on a yellow gold band, a gasp escaped her mouth.

"Joi Ann Lewis, would you be my wife?" He held the box out to her, silently awaiting her reply.

Tears filled her eyes, and she reached out in wonder to touch the ring. In a tear-laden voice, she said, "Yes. Yes."

He got to his feet in a flash, took her hand in his own and slipped the ring onto her trembling finger. As her arms flew around his neck, she heard applause coming from behind her.

Glancing over her shoulder, she saw her entire staff crammed in the doorway leading to the hall. They were cheering, whistling and clapping their hands.

A laughing Joi asked, "How long have y'all been standing there?"

Karen shouted, "Long enough. Now kiss your man, girl!"

Turning her attention back to Marco, she looked into the dark, glittering eyes of the man who would soon become her husband and did as she'd been told.

Epilogue

Joi walked along the strip of sand at Puerto Limón, holding hands with Marco. Returning to this beach, where they'd shared their innermost secrets with each other, felt wonderful. Now that she and Marco were about to make a lifetime commitment, it seemed appropriate to return to the place where she'd first been certain of his place in her life.

Despite it being the first week of December, the weather in Limón was gorgeous. The blue sky above held the bright yellow orb of the sun, unencumbered by clouds as it cast rays of warmth over the sand and water. The temperature was a balmy seventy-eight degrees, a good twenty-five degrees warmer than the day's high back home in Charlotte. She could easily imagine coming here every winter for a vacation, to escape both the city lifestyle and the cool temperatures in the Queen City.

Walking a few steps behind them were Marco's parents, Cruze and Iveliss. Joi and Marco had returned to Limón so that she could meet them, and after having spent the past day and a half in their company, she had to admit she found them delightful. Glancing over her shoulder at them, she smiled when she saw that they were holding hands, as well. Anyone within a one-mile radius of the Alvarezes could see their love for each other, and it was a love Joi aspired to replicate with their son. As in-laws went, she knew she could do a lot worse, and she looked forward to getting to know them even better as time went on.

Marco leaned down, his voice breaking through her thoughts as he spoke into her ear. "You know, I must really love you, to agree to this winter wedding you seem to want so badly. You do know I hate the cold, right?"

She chuckled at his mention of their planned Christmas Eve ceremony, to be held at a large cabin in the mountains of North Carolina. "We'll be inside, so stop whining. Besides, after the ceremony, I'll need you to keep me warm." She leveled him with a sultry gaze, letting her eyes remind him of just how much body heat they were capable of generating.

A low growling sound rumbled up from his throat. "I promise to keep you very warm, Dulce."

He placed a series of soft kisses along her jawline, and her body temperature began to rise. She was so caught up in his kisses that she didn't realize they'd stopped walking until Cruze loudly cleared his throat.

An embarrassed Joi stepped out of the circle of Marco's arms. "Forgive me, Mr. and Mrs. Alvarez."

"Nonsense." Cruze waved off her apology. "You're in love, and there's nothing wrong with that."

A smiling Iveliss added, "Oh yes, dear. We approve, and I'll expect to see some grandchildren very soon."

That only made her blush more.

A grinning Marco pulled her close again. "You heard my parents. We need to get to work right away."

She laughed aloud, until his kiss covered her mouth and stole her breath.

And with the warm breeze flowing around them, she melted into his strong arms and let his kiss whisk her away to paradise.

* * * * *

REQUEST YOUR FREE BOOKS!

2 FREE NOVELS
PLUS 2 FREE GIFTS!

KIMANI™
ROMANCE

Love's ultimate destination!

JUST CAN'T GET ENOUGH?

Join our social communities
and talk to us online.

You will have access to the latest
news on upcoming titles and special
promotions, but most importantly,
you can talk to other fans about your
favorite Harlequin reads.

Harlequin.com/Community

Facebook.com/HarlequinBooks

Twitter.com/HarlequinBooks

Pinterest.com/HarlequinBooks

Her back was to the window and Gray moved to stand
in front of her. He rubbed the backs of his fingers lightly
over her cheek.

"Those buildings mean something to you, don't they?"
he asked her.

She shrugged, shifting from one foot to the other as if
his proximity was making her nervous. Being this close
to her was making him hot and aroused. He wondered if
that was what she was really feeling, as well.

"This town means something to me. There are good
people here and we're trying to do good things."

"That's what my mother used to say," Gray continued, loving the feel of her smooth skin beneath his touch. "Temptation was a good place. Love, family, loyalty. They meant something to the town. Always. That's what she used to tell us when we were young. But that was after the show, after my father found something better outside of this precious town of Temptation."

Gray could hear the sting to his tone, felt the tensing of his muscles that came each time he thought about Theodor Taylor and all that he'd done to his family. Yes, Gray had buried his father two months ago. He'd followed the old man's wishes right down to the ornate gold handles on the slate-gray casket, but Gray still hated him. He still despised any man that could walk away from his family without ever looking back.

"Show me something better," he found himself saying as he stared down into Morgan's light brown eyes. "Show me what this town is really about and maybe I'll reconsider selling."

"Are you making a bargain with me?" she asked. "Because if you are, I don't know what to say. I'm not used to wheeling and dealing big businessmen like you."

"I'm asking you to give me a reason why I shouldn't sell those buildings. Just one will do. If you can convince me—"

She was already shaking her head. "I won't sleep with you, if that's what you mean by *convince* you."

Don't miss ONE MISTLETOE WISH
by A.C. Arthur, available December 2016
wherever Harlequin® Kimani Romance™
books and ebooks are sold.